www.HarperLin.com

A Hiss-tory of Magic

A Wonder Cats Mystery
Book 1

Harper Lin

This is a work of fiction. Names, characters, organizations,places, events, and incidents are either products of the author's imagination or are used fictitiously.

ISBN-13: 978-1987859164
ISBN-10: 1987859162

Contents

1. A Family of Secrets

I definitely should not be writing this down. It's private. Not secret—no. I didn't do anything wrong—at least, not in my opinion. It's been crazy and surreal. You would think that as a witch, I would be used to this kind of thing by now.

As I said, this whole experience is personal, for me alone to deal with, but I really need to let it out, you know? I can't just keep pretending that my life is normal, especially ever since this new hot mess blew up—literally.

I'm trying to make sense of all this, but I don't know where to begin, and my cat keeps trying to use my open notebook as a bed when the cat bed is right there in the corner. Now he's using my wrist as a pillow.

I'm thirty-three years old, and I don't know half of what I should about my own family.

Mystery. That's the word I'm looking for. Detective Williams just calls it a "case" and files it away neatly, but I think his partner knows a mystery when he sees one.

My entire life has been a mystery. I don't know how to explain to myself the secrets that my family has kept all these years... let alone untangling them for nonwitches.

Also, there's the mystery of Ted Lanier and his vegan poutine, which tasted better than the real thing—why didn't we appreciate him more back when he was still with us?

What about the mystery of Min Park? How could he have changed so much as a person? He felt like both the old friend I had known, whom I could spend hours playing games with, and an entirely different person at the same time. Do millionaire entrepreneurs play video games?

The biggest mystery of all is my family. Some mysteries should remain hidden in the mists. This is "the wonderful town of Wonder Falls," after all.

My cousin and soul sister Bea could describe Wonder Falls better than I ever could. She's a lot more like her hippie mother than she thinks, and she's always getting on me to stop and smell the flowers blooming in the crisp Canadian springtime, to go with her on camping and fishing trips by the lake, and to see the waterfalls that the lake runs into.

The waterfalls are magnificent. Of course, they're big. Loud. Damp, eventually. There are three of them, and they generate enough electricity to power the whole town. Tourists come for miles just to look. As for me—well, I live close enough that I've just gotten used to them.

No, no, scratch that. I was getting nostalgic about the way things used to be. Actually, I might never look at the falls the same way ever again.

My name is Cath Greenstone, and I'm a witch.

All the women in the Greenstone family line are witches.

Bea's hippie mother—my Aunt Astrid—owns the best café in town, the Brew-Ha-Ha. Bea and I grew up learning how to run it, and—I write this with all the love in the world for my beautiful and wise Aunt Astrid, who took me in after my parents died—Bea and I both think we'd run it a little differently than Aunt Astrid has.

The fact that we're witches is supposed to be a big secret, but Aunt Astrid is convinced that the best way to go about things is to hide in plain sight. She does fortune-telling for customers, and she talks a lot about the way "mystical energy" moves through the Universe. Yes, Aunt

Astrid uses a capital U, and you can practically hear it when she pronounces the word.

Most of the time, I fear she's daring people to discover us. On a good day—and we'd been having so many good days until the fire—it's reassuring to know that Aunt Astrid has been a witch for longer than all the years Bea and I have spent on this earth combined.

Aunt Astrid can see the future, which is probably the best magical talent a witch can have because a muddy future can be dangerous and painful.

Speaking of "dangerous and painful," Bea's got injury and illness covered with *her* witchy magical talent, which is more easily concealed. People just assume that Bea's a naturally touchy-feely person. Then when they heal quickly, they don't make the connection that Bea had a hand in it and just assume they were going to get healthy again anyway.

It helps to know how the human body works, of course, so Bea's done a lot of reading on that. She's really smart, and she loves to study. She could have left Wonder Falls to go to university and come back with half a dozen Nobel Prizes, never mind a medical degree. Instead, she married Jake and took his name.

I didn't mean that to sound judgmental. Bea's not just my family—she's my best friend. Did I mention she was smart? I wasn't exaggerating. Well, as long as she's happy, I know her talents aren't going to waste.

Jake's a good guy, and everyone in town can't help but like him. He's a good detective too, at least for the quiet, small town of Wonder Falls. However, he hasn't detected that the Greenstone heritage involves magic powers and, therefore, his wife is a witch.

I can communicate with animals, especially cats. I was scared of my own special magical talent at first. Now that I'm older, I really appreciate being able to communicate with Treacle, who's become my best friend, next to Bea.

My skill certainly came in handy on the night of the fire.

2. Treacle's Warning

T reacle is a street cat. I picked him up from the animal shelter run by old Murray Willis. Treacle has a scar on his forehead, probably from a fight with another animal. It has healed into a shiny white welt in the shape of a star, and I doubt fur is ever going to grow over it again.

Whatever incident caused the big scar hasn't stopped Treacle from wandering at night. Neither has the fact that I took him in. I would've preferred that he didn't wander, but it's what he likes to do. Also, he's a black cat, so I worry that he'll find himself under the wheel of a car belonging to a driver that can't see him in the dark.

He'd call me if it happened. Not with a phone—I mean he'd call out to my mind, and distance wouldn't matter. We've got a telepathic bond now, and the communication is getting stronger all the time, but I still worry.

Treacle doesn't speak Human. I speak Cat. It's more of a mind-to-mind magical communication using ideas and images, not so much actual words. That's how I accidentally taught Treacle how to unbolt the cat door.

You'd think I'd have an easier time communicating mind-to-mind with humans because I'm human myself, but even with Bea, it doesn't come naturally—or at all, except under special circumstances. On the rare occasions that telepathic communication with women does work, I need several days to recover. Yes, magic can take a lot out of you. That's something they rarely depict in movies.

Anyway, that was how I knew where Treacle was the night he saw the Brew-Ha-Ha on fire. He got scared and bounded all the way back home at full speed.

When it was barely dawn, whatever I'd been dreaming was interrupted by a fiery nightmare as Treacle shouted into my mind, but I only woke up when he leapt onto the bed and started nipping at my face.

A full understanding of what had happened bypassed my conscious mind and got my instincts going. I jumped out of bed and grabbed the phone on the nightstand.

I was barely awake, completely panicking, and I almost let slip to the 9-1-1 dispatcher that I'd learned about the fire from my cat.

I cleared my throat of its early-morning roughness, shook off the just-woken-up mist from my mind, and tried again. "I can see it from my window," I lied. "That's my aunt's café, for sure, on fire. No, it hasn't spread to any other building yet, but please hurry."

I gave them the address of the café as I stretched the phone cord across the room, straining to reach into my closet to grab something to wear. The line snapped from its socket just as I finished talking.

Treacle nuzzled my ankle then pressed his head into it, purring anxiously.

"Do you think they got it?" I wavered between calling the dispatcher back and getting dressed.

Treacle pawed and nosed the closet door ajar and said, *"I can ask Marshmallow what's going on."*

Marshmallow was Aunt Astrid's cat, a Maine Coon. They had a bond, just as Bea and Peanut Butter had a bond. Marshmallow could even do some magic. When it came to communicating with the cats, however, it was pretty ordinary guesswork between human and cat for Aunt

Astrid and Bea. The cats could talk with each other, and I could talk to the cats.

When they've bonded, as Treacle had with Marshmallow, then distance doesn't matter. So Treacle didn't need to go over to Aunt Astrid's place to check with Marshmallow and then come back to help me decide what to do.

Having a network of minds and being able to communicate instantly can be handy at times, as you might imagine. Although I'm a witch, I'm also a human, so if I do it too much or if I do it with someone whom I haven't formed strong bonds with, then I get headaches. Sometimes my attempts fail, and I only end up receiving mental static, or whichever animal I'm sending my thoughts to just doesn't understand clearly.

Treacle sent to my mind an image of Aunt Astrid in her bedroom. She was fully dressed except for shoes. The image was from the height of Aunt Astrid's ankle, looking up—Marshmallow's point of view.

Aunt Astrid's pear-shaped, slightly overweight figure was very well suited to her billowing drawstring peasant tops and gypsy skirts. Her hair had always been wispy and had never darkened from the dishwater blond of her younger days, although it was beginning to thin. She refused to dye over the pale streaks of gray.

That morning, she'd styled her hair into a French braid, but the locks still loosely framed her face like an ethereal halo. Aunt Astrid had a friendly face. The wrinkles around her mouth and blue eyes bespoke a lifetime of smiling and laughter—in spite of many tragedies.

I felt the ghost of a shift under my elbow as Aunt Astrid eased a pair of canvas flats out from under the giant Maine Coon. She brushed some strands of fur from the shoes before slipping her feet into them.

"You need another grooming," Aunt Astrid said to Marshmallow. "Just as well that there won't be any work today, I suppose, just dealing with the firemen. I'll be back soon."

The image faded. Aunt Astrid knew about the fire.

Treacle leapt to the windowsill, flicked his tail, and meowed. He didn't like fires. I wondered right then if that had something to do with how he'd gotten that star-shaped scar on his forehead. Treacle didn't want to think about it to himself, let alone to me. The fire at the Brew-Ha-Ha had spoiled his morning, and he just wanted to take a nap.

"I might as well go since I'm already up. It will just be insurance stuff and renovating the place, then," I said to myself. "No need to wake Bea, too."

I relaxed too soon, thinking that one of the perks of having an oracular aunt was being able to get a heads-up at times like that. As I said, I don't know half of what I should by now about magic. Every time you think you're in control of your powers or your circumstances, something comes at you from left field.

Nothing could have prepared my family for that morning.

3. The Humorless Detective

On a bench across the street from the Brew-Ha-Ha, I sat myself down beside Aunt Astrid. Wordlessly, Aunt Astrid nudged a paper bag toward me. I uncapped a large thermos I'd brought, poured some strong black tea into the cap, and passed it to Aunt Astrid. Then I poured myself some tea in the smaller, nested plastic cup that came with the thermos, and I reached into the paper bag for one of Astrid's homemade maple bran muffins. Aunt Astrid sipped her tea and sighed. I rubbed my eyes with the back of one hand and stifled a yawn.

Between the bench and the café, a fire truck's siren wailed in the otherwise peaceful morning.

The warm glow of the dawn light had stiff competition from the pillars of lurid flames.

Wonder Falls was so small I recognized most of the firefighters even though I didn't know all of them personally. Gillian Hyllis, the one shouting orders to coordinate the firefighting effort, had come from a family of elitist academics, whom she'd disappointed by following her passion into a more practical profession. Reuben Connors, who rushed to the scene without his gear, was an actual disappointment to the profession.

At the fire hydrant, lining up the hose, was one quarter of the town's support group for divorced fathers and one third of the town's support group for alcoholism recovery, Wayne Walter. I only knew him by name because he had the distinction of attending both groups. From the look of his hosing skills, he was on the ball. That was good to see. Gossip can be vicious, but I think most townsfolk, like me, were silently rooting for him to get his life back on track.

What a relief to see that most of the Wonder Falls fire brigade were in their best shape and getting their jobs done despite generally being unused to having to do them.

Eventually, some of our regular customers passed by and stopped to watch the fire. Some chatted with the firefighters, asking them for details. A few approached Aunt Astrid and me at the bench.

"...all right, there?" The wiry, petite woman spoke so softly that I caught only the end of her sentence.

I managed a smile. "No need to worry about us, Mrs. Park."

"If there's anything you need..."

I'd know where to reach her. We lived in a small town.

That didn't mean everybody was friendly, however. After Mrs. Park wandered off, another figure cut into my line of vision. She had a loud, wheedling voice and smelled of artificial jasmine.

"I had a meeting scheduled here for later this morning!" she huffed.

A skittish part of me remembered my sixth grade again, and I flinched back a bit from the verbal bludgeon of entitlement that was Darla Castellan. Some schoolyard bullies never grew up. I remembered the names she used to call me and how she could manipulate the other kids into following her lead.

Aunt Astrid seemed to have woken up a bit. "I know," she exclaimed. "This is so inconvenient for everybody." She repeated, as a not-so-subtle reminder, "Everybody!"

Darla folded her arms over her chest. "Well, what are you going to do now?"

I took a gulp of tea and shrugged. "Apologize for the inconvenience?"

"And thank you for your continued patronage after we restore the Brew-Ha-Ha," Aunt Astrid said dryly. "It will take a few days."

Part of the café roof collapsed, sending fire-fighters scurrying to herd the spectators away, to a safer distance.

"Weeks," Aunt Astrid corrected. "A month, at the most."

"Continued patronage," Darla scoffed, "is an awfully big presumption." She stormed off in a huff. When she decided to snub or shun somebody, she meant it.

"Genius," I said, clinking Aunt Astrid's teacup with mine.

The residents of Wonder Falls loved the Brew-Ha-Ha—the location, the architecture (so we'd keep it as close to the original as possible when rebuilding the place, I thought), the impeccably polite staff, and the baked goods only a genuine French chef could make.

"Oh!" I gasped and realized aloud, "I should have called Ted!" Ted was our baker and cook. He came in to work at the crack of dawn, before everyone else.

"I left him a message on his answering machine," Aunt Astrid assured me. "I told him not to come in today and that we'll handle everything."

Another voice—from behind us, high, sweet, and raspy—added, "I wish I knew that! I called him just now too, but he's not answering."

It was Bea. Her dark-red hair was naturally styled in glossy waves. She'd inherited that from her father, along with the dark eyes. Our maternal grandfather must have been the one responsible for Bea's flawless, almost olive complexion.

"Good morning! I mean, better morning from now on." Bea put an arm around both of us and peered up at the building. "How did this happen?"

The fire had already been extinguished. I caught sight of Jake across the road, shaking hands with one of the firefighters. He glanced toward the three of us and gave something between a wave and a salute. He wasn't usually so cold, but I reasoned that I'd never seen Jake in action, so maybe he steeled up for his police work.

"Well," Aunt Astrid said, "I had a vision of the fire months ago, and since then, I've been so careful. After closing up, I'd see to it that Ted turned the gas off. Everything that had plugs in the wall sockets, I'd unplug myself." She heaved a sigh of resignation. "Sometimes, the future that I see is fixed."

"I refuse to believe that," Bea declared. More quietly, she suggested, "Senior moment yesterday, maybe?"

Aunt Astrid gave a deep belly laugh as I exclaimed, "Bea!"

"Mother knows what I mean. You could have told us. We would have helped. That's all I meant!"

"I don't have senior moments, Bea. I have ascended moments of omniscience."

"You mean precognition."

As they chatted, I watched as Jake intentionally stood between Gillian and a man I hadn't seen before. He couldn't have just been a visitor in town, judging from how Jake and the firefighter were both acting so tense. The strange man's strikingly handsome face was ruined by a squint when he turned and caught my eye. I returned his glower with an expression of confused stubbornness. Still, I didn't look away. Jake gave him a sharp word, and the strange man broke eye contact with me to acknowledge the argument he was almost having with Jake.

"That's Blake Samberg. He studied forensics in Boston," Bea told me. "He's Jake's new partner, been so these past two and a half weeks."

Aunt Astrid hummed as she considered the two men. "They seem to be getting along."

"Jake complains a lot about how on edge Blake is. City slickers, you know." Bea rolled her eyes. "I bet he's accusing the firefighters of arson. He calls it his gut, but really he's just conditioned to be extra suspicious of absolutely everybody else in the world."

"What a shame," I said. "He's cute."

Bea drawled, "Give it time." She waggled her eyebrows at me. "Either he'll have you on edge too, or—"

"Wonder Falls will mellow him out." Aunt Astrid finished, confidently. She handed the thermos cap back to me and carefully folded up the empty paper bag.

As the fire truck began to pull away, Blake and Jake entered the ruins of the café, and Bea urged us off the bench to gather materials for the cleanup. She had the keys to her minivan, where the cleaning supplies waited.

The sun should've been up at that time of the morning, but the light from the overcast sky wasn't brightening the scene very much. "I hope it doesn't rain. The Brew-Ha-Ha doesn't have a roof anymore."

"Not over the customer area. We can go check on the kitchen." Aunt Astrid stood up to go, and Bea and I followed.

We went around back and met Jake on his way out.

"Don't go in there." Jake's voice was stern, his expression worried, with a hint of panic.

Bea looked confused for a moment. "What, do you think I had so much sentimental attachment to this café?" she asked with a laugh. "These things happen, sweetheart. We just do our best with whatever happens in business." Then she moved toward the kitchen anyway.

Jake interrupted her with a grappling sort of hug, trying to turn his wife away.

He was too late. Bea saw something inside the kitchen and screamed.

Blake strode up to the back entrance and blocked the way through.

"What is it?" I demanded of him.

Aunt Astrid handed me her broom and put her hands on her hips. "What is going on here?"

"This is a crime scene. Please"—Blake gestured toward the sidewalk—"wait here until we can call for backup." His voice was hoarse and deeper than I'd expected for someone with such a clean-cut look.

Aunt Astrid and I exchanged startled looks.

Arson. Some troubled teenager left rude vandalism that survived the building fire.

Bea, still in Jake's embrace, sobbed. She wouldn't have shed tears over a bit of vandalism.

"Wh—who was that?" she asked.

"We don't know yet," Jake answered at the same time that Blake said, "Théodore Lanier."

"Damn it, Samberg!"

I'd never heard Jake swear before.

"Ted?" I could barely get the name out. My nerves trembled with the looming sensation of something gone very, very wrong. "Théodore's his full name, Théodore Lanier." It's supposed to be pronounced "lan-YAY" in that Frenchy way, where the R is silent. "He's our baker. What about him?"

Blake turned to me again. "If the driver's license belonged to the body, ma'am, then it could very well be that Ted... is dead."

Aunt Astrid gasped in horror.

"There's a body in there, burnt to a crisp. Your baker's been roasted," Blake deadpanned.

Jake's jaw dropped. Bea released a wailing sob.

"Mr. Lanier"—Blake mispronounced the name "LANE-ee-yur"—"could now be that body that's layin' 'ere."

I squeezed my eyes shut and held up my palm toward Blake, to stop him. "I've got the gist of it, yeah! Detective… Punster, is it?"

"Do you think I have a sense of humor?" Blake growled the question, seeming offended.

I seethed. "I'll take any explanation other than the answer that this is really happening."

"We've got procedures to follow now," Jake said. "Samberg's right, at least on the point that this is a crime scene. We need backup to investigate before we know more."

He rubbed Bea's arm to comfort her. They walked back to the police car, and the rest of us followed.

I didn't notice it then, but Marshmallow must have darted from the alleyway at that moment and followed us.

4. A Lesson in Magic

Marshmallow later told me what had lured her out. I'll do my best to translate, beginning with the moment Aunt Astrid left that morning. Before I get to that, though, I need to explain something about witchcraft.

Basically, witches work with another dimension. Most people know that dimensions consist of height, breadth, and depth. Some people consider the passage of time the fourth dimension, and I don't know if that's true because I'm not a physicist, but that sure would make the next thing I'm going to explain a little easier to grasp.

The other dimension exists. It's obvious to us witches. We balance that world with the life in this world, which we share with nonwitches.

Imagine a square. Now, notice how a square can turn into a cube with an added dimension or just a few extra lines to suggest it. Time takes a different shape too, with an added dimension or two or three or more. That's why Aunt Astrid experiences time out of order: she lives the future in the present.

Every person, even nonwitches, has an extra body in this collection of other dimensions. It interfaces with one's physical body, locked to it for as long as life continues.

The bodies of the other dimensions get damaged more easily but heal more quickly than physical bodies, but because of the interface, the state of one body does affect the other. That's how Bea does her healing. Her body in the other dimension has a looser interface with her own, and her witchy senses let her see exactly what is wrong with the other person's "other" body. She works her magic, which these other dimensions are made out of, and she makes people healthy again or at least takes away their pain.

Cats know the other dimensions even better than witches do. I just happen to be in the same zone most cats are in, which is why I can connect with cats better than Bea or Aunt Astrid.

These other dimensions are like an ocean. It has zones of visibility, currents, quakes, and an irregular ebb and flow that makes it difficult to explore. That's why we witches have different talents from each other and also why a single talent might not work all the time.

Practicing witchcraft is like sailing a ship on an ocean. We can set down an anchor, as Bea can do with healing people's bodies; we can tether to a buoy, as I do with the bonds I make with cats; we can turn the sails when the wind changes, as Aunt Astrid tries to do in response to her visions of the future. However, if there's a giant tidal wave or an iceberg or a sea monster… Well, then it's all we can do to keep from sinking. When that happens, witches and nonwitches are in the same boat, really.

Okay, maybe not. We witches do our best, but that has never been good enough for nonwitches. Nonwitches have always thought that just because we know when some danger from another dimension is coming, we're also dangerous—that, because we're not strong enough to stop evil, we must be evil, too. No wonder we're neurotic about our privacy!

The Greenstones came to Ontario from Massachusetts. My I-don't-know-how-many-greats grandmother took the hint from the witch trials in Salem that the New World still had old problems. She might have run forever but never found a place where a witch could be accepted by other human beings.

She settled in Ontario because she found acceptance here from a being that's never been human. Among the generations of Greenstone women since then, this being has been known as the Maid of the Mist.

When I was at that awkward and insecure age of dealing with bullies at school—and growing into a magical talent I couldn't accept because magic had left me orphaned—I took frequent trips to the waterfalls where the Maid of the Mist was supposed to have first appeared to the errant Greenstones.

I'd been full of hope that the Maid of the Mist would appear to me and grant me some guidance, but she never did. Maybe she wasn't as connected to us witches as we'd thought. Or maybe the Maid of the Mist just wasn't interested in the emotional issues of adolescent humans.

But on the day of the fire, the Maid of the Mist appeared to Marshmallow.

5. Marshmallow Moans

I didn't want a grooming. *I might like that it takes me back to my days in show, during which I won ribbons and was very proud to look so pretty, but that time is past. It's for no good reason now that Astrid takes me to that cold, bright place to get rained on, and I don't taste right afterward when I try to clean myself. Sometimes I get indigestion from whatever they put in my fur. I'm getting too old for grooming.*

Yet I'm also too old to fight, scratch, and bite in protest. Besides, I know it will be over sooner if I don't make any trouble.

When the time came, instead of taking me to the groomer's, Astrid said she was going somewhere and told me to stay put. I took a catnap. Instead of being at the groomers for real, I had an uncomfortable dream about the grooming, a nightmare.

I wasn't sure if I was still dreaming when I heard a hissing sound. It made me curious because it was half like the sound of the rain that humans make and half like the sound of a cat warning everybody else away. Usually, I don't care, but this was a voice that knew me, and it wanted help.

I opened my eyes. I didn't know if the sound had woken me up or if I was still dreaming, but the room of the grooming salon disappeared and made way for a vast dreamscape of open sky and wild river waters. At what felt like the end of the earth, the wide river dropped. The hiss became a roar of water hitting water that made my fur fluff up with fright. I had already gotten wet and didn't want to drown.

Then I saw the falling water take the shape of a cat. She was a long-haired Persian—or at least she was shaped like one—but I think that was just a shape that she was taking so that I could understand her.

She told me that Astrid Greenstone should take "it" from her—but that she needed the other humans to help—and me, too.

"You have the wrong cat. I don't know the streets," I told her. "If they don't come fetch me, then I can't help them. I'm too old for this."

The Cat of the Mist told me, "No, it has to be you. Treacle can help get you there. Hurry, or else—"

I challenged her: "Or else what? What gave you the right to threaten me with anything?"

The Cat of the Mist turned into mist that wasn't shaped like anything, and I dreamed that the water covered where this giant misty cat used to be. It overflowed over everything. The bank of the river broke with all the water, which then filled the forest even to the top of the trees. I saw this as if I wasn't really there, as though I was flying. The dream changed so that I was in it instead of only watching, but the overflow didn't stop. I clung onto a branch, feeling like a kitten again, when I used to play in trees, climb too high, and get stuck.

I woke up.

The window was open because I never sneak out and sometimes Treacle sneaks in. I jumped out the window, leaving the cool and cozy familiar smells of my home.

I sent Treacle a message: "I'm outside. Now where do I go?"

Treacle was astonished. "Outside? You? Without a human?"

"I'm going to get to a human if you would just tell me. I'll tell you why later. I don't want to be late."

Treacle gave me some roundabout directions because he wanted me to stay away from the street gangs. When I understood where our humans would be, I ignored the detour and passed through street-gang territory to get there. Do you know, now, how much I put myself through for you?

Really, they weren't that bad. I'm a big cat, and my fur makes me look even bigger and tougher. If I moved right, they wouldn't even notice I was old. They were mostly surprised to see a strange new cat that they didn't know.

I didn't run, in case that would make them curious enough to chase me. One rude young calico that smelled like the Dumpster tried to rally the others to corner me, but many of them had stayed up all night hunting and weren't in a mood for surprises.

I could have used magic then. Not all cats can do it. Two things stopped me: First, I knew the magic would leave me for the next hour if I used it then. Second, I knew my humans would need my magic.

What was really bad was the dog out walking its human.

Oh, the dogs!

Dogs you should run from when they see you because they're loud and violent first. They don't think. They're not smart enough, not like cats. Humans only think that dogs are smarter because dogs are more likely to do as they're told. And even so, they don't do that all the time.

This one's human made noises like "No!" and "Come back!" after the giant St. Bernard broke the strap that kept them together. I had to run, duck into an alleyway, and climb over a wire fence. At my age, too!

I very much wanted to use magic then too, but I didn't.

When I finally found my human, Astrid, you can imagine my relief. I wasn't done yet, of course. The gods are annoying.

Five humans walked out to the banks of a dry river made of rough flagstones. I didn't know one of them, the one who was asking, "Did Mr. Lanier have any reason to come in early?"

Astrid answered, "Work ethic—that's the only thing I can think of. I had no idea he would come in so early, but he does that sometimes—or he did, if that corpse is really his. Oh, how awful!"

"He loved his job," Cath said. "A kitchen accident..." She shook her head. "That would have been a bad way to go."

The human I didn't know said, "We don't know enough to say that it was an accident yet."

Astrid and Cath stepped away from him, and my human said, "Just what are you implying?"

"Just that the police will be wondering what you could have done, too. It's our job."

I didn't like him. He was making my humans unhappy, so I ran in front of his ankle to trip him.

He stumbled. "What?" Then his voice sounded pleased. "Oh, what a pretty kitty!"

I gave him an annoyed sideways-and-upward glance as he ruffled the fur at the top of my head.

"And she's friendly! It is a she, right?"

"Yes," my human confirmed. I meowed up at her.

"This is yours?" The strange human picked me up comfortably, grasping my ribs behind my forelegs not too tightly, then putting an arm under my hind legs. I relaxed like a rag-doll cat, but when he had me against his suit, I pawed to show that I still didn't like him. His suit smelled like catnip. I don't care because I'm one of the rare cats that catnip does nothing for, but I wondered how much he actually liked cats.

"I was going to take her to the grooming salon," Astrid said to him, taking me from his arms. "Marshmallow must have escaped from Bea's car. I'll take her back now."

Astrid was lying to him for some reason.

"And these won't be needed for a while, either," Cath added, lifting the bucket of hay on a stick and the rope monster on a stick.

Treacle and even Peanut Butter liked to chase after the hay. I didn't. None of us liked the rope monster because it was usually damp and smelled too sharp and gross.

The strange human said, "Let me help you with that—"

"No, I can manage," Cath told him. "Shouldn't you be calling for backup? Jake's a little tied up right now, what with being a decent human being to his wife, and you've got to delegate the real work of investigation to other people so that you can make your accusations."

Astrid was holding me up to her shoulder, so as they walked away, I saw the strange male human's crestfallen expression.

Cats have sharp ears, and I heard him say, "I'm just doing my job..." And he walked away.

"We hadn't brought Marshmallow with us," Cath whispered. "Wouldn't he have noticed?"

"For now, we've got a more critical problem," Astrid whispered back. "We need to get back in there before backup comes."

Cath is a good listener. I told her, I can hide you— with magic, I can do it. None of the other humans will know that you were ever there.

Still, she was confused. "Why? What—and Marsh-mallow just volunteered to do her magic."

That's what I went there for.

"That's going to be a big spell," Astrid said. "It would be easier with Bea, but we need to be discreet, and we need to do it now."

We arrived at Bea's moving machine, which they called a "car," though it wasn't moving then.

Cath opened the door and pushed the things she was carrying into the car. She said, "Aunt Astrid, you're scaring me. What's going on?"

Cath knows about big spells, dangerous spells. She should have been allowed to go the rest of her life without being exposed to the dangerous repercussions of magic again.

"It's faster to show you," Astrid told her, as she moved me from her shoulder onto the cushioned surface covering the inside of Bea's moving machine. "And we do need to be fast."

Cath gave something like a human version of an anxious meow, then she surrendered. "All right. How do we do this?"

Cats can shift between this world, that world, and the other. We don't normally take up the gatekeeper role, but my human is a witch, so I did that. That's why I can use magic. Treacle and Peanut Butter are too young to do it like I can.

We cast three large spells. They would be a stretch of the two humans' usual talents. First, I would need to pull the other dimension over this one. Doing that would make witchcraft easier for my humans to do, but even then, the spell would not be easy.

Cath would pull some of this dimension around the dimension I pulled so that anybody nearby would not be able to pay attention to them, would not be able to remember, and would not even know they'd forgotten anything when the two ended the spell and joined the solid world again. That part would come from Cath's talent with minds even though she had never played with the mind of a human before and wouldn't want to do it ever again.

My human would do the same kind of magic, except with time. Any marks they left, footprints or strands of hair, would stay missing in that place until three days later. That would come from her talent with time and could work because the future is mostly not set.

None of those effects were normal manifestations of our usual powers. Casting those spells was going to be difficult for all of us.

6. The Time Travelers

I was afraid I was going to die. Marshmallow and Aunt Astrid were obviously both worried that they wouldn't be able to pull the magic off, but still, they had a quiet determination that came from knowing why they would have to try in the first place. I didn't have that, and I still had to do a big spell—my first big spell since witnessing the one that took both my parents away from me.

When Marshmallow started to pull the other dimension—or some magic from the other dimension—in over this one, I felt like a little kid again, watching the monster come out from under my bed and feeling helpless as my mom tried to keep it at bay by waving her quartz-crystal wand. She'd drawn a protective circle on my bedroom floor and told me not to leave it. My dad had run into the room—

I forced myself to focus, telling myself, *That was then and this is now.* No evil beings were exploding out of a portal—we were just making a phenomenal effort to tweak people's minds.

Besides, Aunt Astrid was the one who had to do the magical heavy lifting, moving us into the Brew-Ha-Ha of the future just enough that we wouldn't leave a trace in it in the present but not enough to cause some temporal paradox that would collapse every dimension in on itself.

That wasn't as comforting a thought as I'd wanted it to be. First of all, a big spell was a big spell. Second of all, I wondered if we could really end the world by casting it. Bea would know the risks better because she reads about quantum physics. Aunt Astrid was just convinced that it was worth the risk.

Anyway, Marshmallow began to let the other worlds into our default one.

The sensation of that happening felt a little bit like standing under a waterfall as the numbingly cold water beats down on the top of your head. I forced myself to open my eyes against that flux and to move forward.

Aunt Astrid and I began to walk to the back entrance of the Brew-Ha-Ha. Bea caught sight of us, cloaked in magic. Jake turned toward us, and my breath caught, but he looked right through us and returned his attention to Bea, to my relief. Blake was in the police car, speaking into the two-way radio. He didn't take any notice of us either.

I gritted my teeth against the waves of magic as Aunt Astrid began to fold time in on itself. I saw a corpse in the kitchen with the same height and buff build that Ted had. As we took the next step, the body faded into a chalk outline, and in another step, it had become clean, new tiling. I began to feel dizzy.

Aunt Astrid led the way out of the kitchen and behind the bar, which was badly burnt but still standing. Behind the bar was a trapdoor. Aunt Astrid pulled it open just enough to squeeze through and make her way down to the stairs below. The trapdoor remained open at an angle that would have been physically impossible to maintain if it weren't frozen in time.

As I was about to follow, something on the ground caught my eye. It was a pendant on a chain, glinting silver against the soot and char. Because of the time manipulation, it flickered in and out of existence, but something about that necklace burned against the magic.

It could only do that if it were magic itself.

I took my phone out of my pocket and snapped a few pictures of the pendant. I don't know how physics and technology work when they're mixed with magic. Maybe Bea's developed some grand unifying theory, but I just do what I hope works out well in the end.

"Cath?" Aunt Astrid called.

I snatched the necklace from the ground, pocketed it, and then followed Aunt Astrid downstairs into the cellar.

The magic faded as we reached the bottom of the stairs. I leaned on the railing and waited for my nausea to pass.

"Marshmallow should keep the spell going on above us." Aunt Astrid's voice sounded frail in the pitch darkness. "I built this basement to stand up against a nuclear war. Fire wouldn't have touched it."

With a click, a flashlight flickered to life, the silver beam of light illuminating the room. It was a bunker—gray, concrete, and bare except for a shelf of dusty canned goods. I felt as if I hadn't slept in days. That's what magic burnout does to a person, and we were only halfway done.

"What was so important that we had to do this?" I groaned miserably.

Aunt Astrid beckoned and handed me the flashlight. "Hold this for a moment."

I shone it at the corner she was approaching.

"I needed to keep something here that was very important," Aunt Astrid told me as she opened one of the fuse boxes. "It's a spell book that we've kept in our family for generations. You know the spell that we're casting now? It's a cantrip compared to the weakest spell in that book."

She wrenched back a panel of switches and wires—a false display. I held my breath as she reached into the back of the fake fuse box.

She drew her hand back and exhaled sharply. "It's gone. Someone's taken it."

"Who would do that?" I asked, but I knew the answer to that. "Somebody who wants to do magic more powerful than we're doing."

"Somebody," Aunt Astrid added, "who knows that we kept it. Somebody who knows that we're witches."

I gulped. What could have given us away? We'd all been so careful, and Wonder Falls was such a safe town.

"Turn the light onto the floor."

I jumped back, startled, when I saw faint footprints leading from the stairs to the fuse box.

"Those are new," Aunt Astrid said.

"They don't belong to us," I observed. "The size of the shoe is too big."

I took note of the outsoles' imprints, too. They looked smooth, as though they belonged to formal shoes, not patterned like hiking boots or sneakers.

"Maybe..." My mind spun. "Maybe it was just an eccentric collector. Maybe they'll leave us alone now that they have what they want. It was a family heirloom, sure, but not one that we ever used, so—"

Aunt Astrid muttered a word, and a blast of magic shot out of the fake fuse box. It gave the air a fresh tang, like ozone or Freon.

"Protecting that book is a duty that I take very seriously," Aunt Astrid said as she reached into the fuse box once more. She drew out an old, leather-bound tome. "The thief stole a fake copy. I had this one hidden in a pocket dimension, guarded by the Maid of the Mist." She turned to me and said harshly, "We're all in great danger, Cath. Whoever found this set this whole place on fire, and now Ted is dead. Just remember that."

We made our way back outside to Bea's car, with Aunt Astrid tightly knotting time behind us. We wouldn't want investigators to walk onto the scene, disappear for days, and then reappear, insisting that no time at all had passed for them. We only wanted any evidence that we'd been there moved away somewhere safe.

When all that was done, Marshmallow flicked her ears and tucked the other dimension away, back where it belonged. Aunt Astrid and I raised a sort of magic wall that would prevent magic from coming through even though the wall itself was magic—it's easier to do if you don't think about it too much. I don't usually think about "How?" except when I repeat what Bea's figured out about how it works, but that day I was thinking about "Why?" and "Should we or should we not?"

So I didn't pull the spell off easily. Most magic walls that we cast are actually walls of spells—for example, to make a nonwitch afraid to go near a place for some unexplainable reason. Those walls take a long time to grow, but they tend to stay up for a while. We needed that sort of power in crunch time, which even Aunt Astrid—who had worked with time magic all her life—had difficulty with.

With a final burst of power, I felt the wall align.

Aunt Astrid clapped her hands and looked from Marshmallow to me. "Well done, team!"

I had to lean against Bea's car to keep myself from fainting.

Bea walked briskly over to meet us. "I convinced Jake to take his partner on their beat and interrogate us after."

She still looked visibly shaken by what she'd seen. That much was no act. I gave her a hug. She looked as though she needed it.

As she hugged me back, she sniffled and said, "I want to go home. You can catch me up on whatever you just did when we're there."

"Just don't forget to lock your car doors from now on," Aunt Astrid told her as she got into the driver's seat. "This neighborhood isn't as safe as it used to be."

7. Bea's Books

B ea's house looked more like a library than a home. In every room except the kitchen and bathroom, she had bookshelves instead of walls. The shelves reached the ceiling and had side-rolling ladders mounted on them.

In the kitchen was a trolley—a trolley!—full of books, and they weren't even all cookbooks. I rolled them into the living room.

"I read over those when I have a midnight snack!" Bea objected when she saw me.

"What, all of them at the same time?" I furrowed my brow. "That's impossible. Besides, it's a fire hazard. I'm kind of concerned about that now, you know."

At that, Bea smiled sadly and laid out a serving platter of cold smoked salmon with avocado sauce and toasted crumpets. "When were you going to tell us about that spell book, Mom?"

"It's in my will," Aunt Astrid answered from the sofa, where she sat reading. "If anything happened to me, then it would go to you and Cath—technically. You'd be advised not to move it. You're both talented and intuitive enough that you would've been able to figure out the rest."

Bea munched on a crumpet thoughtfully. "Could the lawyer have caught on that this heirloom spell book was so valuable?"

Peanut Butter hopped up onto the sofa where Marshmallow sat curled up. They sniffed each other's noses and rubbed their heads together.

Aunt Astrid replied, "I only said that it was a book, that it was part of my collection. If it was a spell book of ultimate power, people would expect me to say so."

"My mother," Bea said, flourishing her hand, "master of the triple bluff."

"However, existence of the book got out. Why act on that information only now, though?" I wondered. "This is such a tiny, quiet town. What changed?"

Bea hummed, getting into bookworm mode. "I can only think of two things. First, somebody who was close to us, who could catch every moment that we slipped—who'd catch enough of those moments to wonder if there wasn't more going on—"

"You think Ted did this?" I asked with disbelief.

"Well," Bea said, "that's only one of my thoughts. How nice was the author who wrote the fake book, the one that actually got stolen? Did she write spells that simply wouldn't work, or did she write spells that made sure that whoever tried them wouldn't get a chance to steal the real one? Try to conjure up a magic fireball, and it could backfire and…"

"There would have been a book beside the body," I said.

"And 'whoever thought up the fake spell book' was very nice—a downright tree-hugging hippie, as a matter of fact," Aunt Astrid said, pointing at herself. She shook her head. "I'm sorry, girls. I've only bought us time."

"Don't blame yourself," I told her. "The only one doing anything wrong here is this power-hungry thief, arsonist, and murderer who's meddling in things that not even we completely understand."

Astrid sighed. "I will blame myself if it turns out to be Ted himself—an accomplice might have double-crossed him and made away with the book. Ted didn't like to talk about his family or what was going on in his life, and in the decade he's been with us—I never pried!" Aunt Astrid heaved the spell book back into her bag and joined us at the dining table. Bea poured her mother a lemonade, and Astrid gulped it down.

On the sofa, Peanut Butter and Treacle curled up beside Marshmallow. Treacle could always find a way into the house. Marshmallow also seemed to have been exhausted by the spell.

"It couldn't have been Ted," Aunt Astrid said decisively. "He wasn't interested in magic—not at all. He'd always refuse my astrology readings."

"The other thing I'm thinking," Bea said, "is that it's a newcomer. Maybe a tourist pretending to have come to see the falls."

"Or..." A thought occurred to me, and I spoke it slowly. "A new detective in town, taking the perfect position to try to turn the tables and pin the blame on us?" I remembered the necklace I'd found and took it out of my pocket. "Could this have been a clue? I found it while we were walking through, and I thought it was magical."

Bea peered at it. "Weird, but not magical— not anymore, at least."

"We were covered in magic," Aunt Astrid pointed out. "Maybe you imagined that part."

"It wasn't there when I swept the place up yesterday," I said. "It was charred. This definitely wasn't Ted's."

"Maybe a locator spell—" Bea began, and Aunt Astrid and I interrupted her with synchronized groans of misery. "All right! All right. Not yet. Not like that's any of our talents, anyway."

Aunt Astrid told her, "There are no locator spells in the Greenstone spell book although there are other spells I'm aware of."

"But," I added, "if there were a locator spell in that book... If two out of three of us weren't recovering from magic burnout right now, would we be able to cast a locator spell? What about spells in this book that would help witches so their powers weren't limited to one or two talents?"

Aunt Astrid said, "That would mean that even nonwitches wouldn't be limited. They would have magic as well. The words, the ingredients, the gestures—all were designed to create an intersection between this world and the worlds beyond, no matter what. So, yes, it also means that witches could work outside their talents. You see how important it is to keep this spell book out of the wrong hands."

I sent the clearest pictures of the necklace from my phone to Bea's, and I deleted the rest.

Bea leaned back in her seat. "So, then... All we can do is guess until we know more."

"No," I said. "We need to figure out what's going on. We can't just wait around—not with so much at stake!"

Bea added gloomily, "We're at stake... as witches have a historical tendency to be. Ha ha."

"It will be a witch hunt at best," Aunt Astrid agreed. "At worst... Well, that worst won't happen, not as long as they don't have the book. I'm taking this home with me to personally ensure its safety!"

"We just have to wait until we know more," Bea said. "Do you really want to go home, Mom? Are you sure?"

Aunt Astrid nodded. "The Maid of the Mist is more powerful than the three of us combined, but she wouldn't be able to move the dimension pocket. There are generations of protection spells in the old Greenstone house. That's the second-best option."

"Cath," Bea said, turning to me, "you know, we've got a guest room. You're welcome to stay overnight, and Treacle is, too."

I was just about to protest that the situation wasn't that bad when Treacle spoke into my mind.

"Well," I said instead, "Marshmallow says she's not going anywhere, and Treacle isn't leaving Marshmallow."

"And you don't want to go back to your place alone," Bea finished warmly.

It wasn't until she said it that I realized it was true, never mind what was going on with the cats. I'd inherited my house from my parents. I hardly ever think about what happened there because it was decades ago, but after the big spell that day, going back there would remind me of the monster under my bed.

Most kids have imaginary friends or monsters. In a family line of witches, those imaginary beings usually turn out to be real, which can be pretty disconcerting.

So Bea drove Aunt Astrid back to her place, and I stayed in the guest bedroom.

Bea spent the afternoon making calls and drafting letters to the insurance company, and Treacle kept watch over the sleeping Marshmallow. Peanut Butter pawed at the bottom of the guest room's door until I let him in, and we talked. Yes, I had magic burnout, but I'd guess it's sort of like waiting tables when you feel as though you're about to come down with the flu or feeling as if you've pulled an all-nighter.

Peanut Butter was so insecure that he really needed a chat, so I exerted the effort to do so even though I would be completely drained of magic for the whole next day.

Our talk was mostly just me reassuring Peanut Butter that Jake didn't dislike him and that Bea and Jake weren't going to split up and abandon Peanut Butter in a cardboard box on the side of the road. I told Peanut Butter that the stereotypes humans have about cats being proud and independent just didn't fit him.

Neither Treacle nor I told Peanut Butter about the fire, Ted's death, or the big magical spell.

I did show Peanut Butter the pendant, though. He said it reminded him of the four-sided dice that Jake's nephew and his friends played with.

I remembered those. Min Park, who was Mrs. Park's son, had been a great fan of those fantasy-adventure tabletop roleplaying games when we were back at school. Once Bea's brain ate up all the guidebooks, she became the most annoying player, a total stickler for the rules. She was better at running the game and telling the players what was what than she was at playing. When we tried certain actions, we rolled dice—six-sided, ten-sided, twenty-sided dice—to determine whether the characters we played would succeed or not. The four-sided dice were more painful to step on than Lego bricks.

Of course, those medieval fantasy games had magic, and I might have let it slip once that how we played out magic usage according to the guidebooks wasn't how magic "really" worked. Min Park was a good friend, but I think he dismissed that comment as my taking a fictional entertainment medium too seriously.

I realized then that I hadn't made a lot of friends since Min had left. I hadn't noticed because my family lived nearby, and I wasn't as much of a social butterfly as Bea. Maybe animal communication had spoiled me because, to me, nothing is clearer than a pure thought, a pure emotion, a memory, or a mix of the three just dropped into your mind. I wondered if I could try something new more often—meet new people or meet familiar people in new ways.

All right, maybe I didn't mull over all of that at the time. If I did, it would have been pushed to the back of my mind, considering the much bigger concern about who knew the Greenstone legacy, which we'd tried to keep so private.

When evening fell, Bea fried up some ground turkey and potato wedges. Jake called to say he would be working overtime that night. I gave Marshmallow some of the turkey just to get her to eat something. After taking the afternoon off to rest, I was feeling better, but Marshmallow still felt terrible.

8. The Unusual Suspects

T he next morning, Marshmallow was too sick to get up. We weren't sure if Bea using magic healing for what could be a symptom of magic burnout would make it worse, so Bea took her to the vet, and I took Bea's claim letter to the insurance company's office after Bea told me that we had gotten clearance from the fire inspector. I was still feeling tired, too, and delivering a letter sounded like it would be less trouble.

The next morning, Marshmallow was too sick to get up. We weren't sure if Bea would make it worse by using magical healing for what could be a symptom of magic burnout, so Bea took her to the vet, and I took Bea's claim letter to the insurance company's office after Bea told me we'd gotten clearance from the fire inspector. I was still feeling tired too, and delivering a letter sounded like less trouble.

Oh, if I'd only known!

The rain that had threatened to break the day before had passed. That day, the sun blazed in an uninterrupted expanse of blue sky, and the wind blew just enough to keep the day cool.

Most of the townspeople seemed to be in a great mood that day, whether they were in Old Wonder Falls with the cobblestones and mom-and-pop shops or in the town square with the asphalt and the view of the franchise grocery store and the falls. The same chipper cheer, I imagined, would be prevailing in the fisheries and farms and where the fruit orchards met the forest.

That day, it would have been so nice to be one of those ordinary people instead of pretending to be one, even if I was just filing an insurance claim.

Inside the insurance office, I bumped into Nadia and Naomi LaChance, twin sisters who had been Bea's friends in high school: from mathletes and drama club, respectively. Nadia spoke at a much lower register than Naomi. Nadia had dyed steel-blue hair and a tattoo of a waterfall that blossomed over one shoulder and ran down the length of her arm, all the way to her knuckles.

Naomi—who used wooden pencils to keep her black hair in a bun and wore oversized button-down shirts belted around the waist as if they were dresses (hmm, I should try that out sometime)—was there to get money to repair her car.

Old Mr. Leary, who had driven into the headlight of Naomi's ladybug-patterned Volkswagen Bug the week before, was in the office with Mrs. Sutherland, the insurance agent—well, one of the insurance agents.

I asked if I could talk to someone who wasn't already with a client, and the office assistant—a lanky, swarthy boy in his late teens named Cody, very soft-spoken and formal—directed me to the office of Mr. Nguyen instead.

Cody knocked on the half-open door. "It's Miss Greenstone, sir."

Mr. Nguyen, a hefty man about Aunt Astrid's age, seemed momentarily relieved then tried to muster up some anger, but he wasn't a good actor. He craned his neck past his desk and past the man in the long, dark coat standing in front of him. "Cody, I thought I told you I was in a meeting!"

A familiar, gravelly voice replied, "Oh, no, this is a lucky coincidence. I should be asking you these questions directly"—the figure turned to reveal Blake Samberg—"Cath, isn't it?"

"What are you doing here?" I asked, too tired to be irritated.

"I was just asking Mr. Nungooyen—"

"'Ngwhen,'" Mr. Nguyen interjected.

"—what you stood to gain from a fire at the Brew-Ha-Ha."

I gave him a slow, disdainful blink. "Lost time. Days, maybe weeks, without customers to keep our business going—when, I might add, it was going great—"

"It *was* a very successful business," Mr. Nguyen said, backing me up.

"There goes your insurance fraud theory, Detective." Sarcastically, I added, "What a shrewd use of human resources too, killing our star chef. Great way to run a food business!"

Blake nodded to Mr. Nguyen. "Right." Then he nodded to me. "Thank you both for your time." He made for the door.

As he passed by, I asked, "What, that's it?"

"I believe you." Blake shrugged his shoulders, palms up and out toward me. "We're following every lead in this investigation. I just had to make sure this wasn't one."

And he left.

"Now, you wait just one hot minute!" I left Bea's letter on Mr. Nguyen's desk as Mr. Nguyen signaled desperately at Cody to send the next client in.

Blake Samberg just rubbed me the wrong way. He was presumptuous and insensitive. He wasn't the most unpleasant person I'd ever met, but he sure could find a spot in the top three. I couldn't have been more relieved that he would be out of my sight.

So why was I following him? Why was I stopping him?

Well, I still had questions. "Would you care to update a surviving victim of this crime? What other leads are you talking about?"

Cody lent an arm to old Mr. Cartwright, who had a prosthetic leg—the real one had been lost decades before in a mountain-lion attack—and they hobbled slowly into Mr. Nguyen's office. When the door shut behind them, Blake spared a glance at the LaChance sisters, who tried to look uninterested in our conversation.

"It wasn't asphyxiation," Blake murmured. "No, he burned. The fire started in the oven, and someone made sure that Ted was right in front of it."

I took that information in and exhaled the shock and horror. "Who would do that? Ted was a big, buff guy—who *could* do that?"

"He had a concussion before the fire started. That's a mercy. But someone really wanted to make sure that he was dead. Jake's running a background check on the victim as we speak, to see if he had any enemies back in… Quebec, was it?"

"Or his hometown in France. Only his dad was Canadian. His mother was from… I forgot the name, somewhere in France." *No. This couldn't be personal.* I could only think that Ted had come in early and caught the thief in action. The fire was just a way to get rid of a witness. *Oh, Ted, I'm so sorry you got caught up in this.* "Do you think that someone from his past could have found him without anybody in this town noticing?"

"We have a prime suspect," Blake told me.

"You do?" Every intuitive fiber in my body screamed that he was on the wrong track.

"Does the name Min Park ring a bell?"

The Park family managed the big grocery store that had the view of the falls. Min had gone away for university, and life just got in the way of letter writing. His mother had been at the café on the morning of the fire, making sure that Aunt Astrid and I were okay.

"He's in town?" I hadn't known that.

We used to be very close. My intuition clouded over, embarrassed, and curled up in the corner of my mind like a cat that had missed a mouse.

"In police custody by now—or should be. I got the text message from Jake while I was in Mr. Nguyen's office. Witnesses saw him at the scene of the crime, before the fire."

"No," I said. "No, there must be some mistake. Min Park left Wonder Falls fifteen years ago for university. Ted came to town a couple of years after. They couldn't have met—not here, at least."

Blake got a notebook and pen out of his coat pocket. "Would you testify to his character, then?"

"What's relevant to the case?" I asked. "The Min Park that I knew couldn't wrestle his way out of a wet paper bag. I know this because some schoolyard bullies"—more physical than Darla had been—"once trapped Min in a giant paper bag and threw him into the pool beside the gym. I can't even remember how that happened or why he literally couldn't punch his way out. It was so long ago."

"It was a long time ago," Blake agreed, scribbling something on his notepad.

I insisted, "Min didn't do this. I knew him in grade school. He's a good person."

"Well," Blake said as he folded his notepad again and pocketed it, "most people are good people in grade school. I'm not saying there aren't bad seeds, but life is hard for everybody."

I couldn't imagine Ted and Min facing each other down—what, in some gun duel at high noon, somewhere in the Mexican desert, with their cowboy hats on? *Ted's bullet grazes Min, who falls with a shout and plays dead as Ted saunters away in his chaps and boots. Min's fallen cowboy hat rolls away like the tumbleweed in the breeze, and then when he's sure Ted's gone, he picks himself up, clutching his wound, looks to the sky, and swears vengeance—*

Okay, maybe I could imagine it, but obviously that didn't mean anything like it could have really happened. It just meant I was weird and crazy.

"I have to interrogate him anyway, now—just to be sure." Blake said, bringing me back to earth. "You've convinced me of your innocence. That only works on you. Do you understand?"

He delivered the last line with such grimness that I had to meet the sharpness and challenge of his gaze, and I wondered when I would get sick of our staring contests. "No," I answered.

"This is about my family, my friends, in my hometown and my life. I don't fight just for my own innocence and protection. I fight for everyone's!"

"Good," Blake said, with a shade of... disappointment or maybe worry. "I'll just make sure that they're worthy of your loyalty."

"How can you possibly make sure of that?"

"It's my job. I work with the proof." He turned to walk out.

I almost stopped him, but I caught sight of Nadia's girlfriend coming down the hall. It was Ruby Connors, who'd been Darla's best friend at school, and—judging by her tailored blazer, hot-pink plaid A-line skirt, and stiletto heels—they still went shopping together.

I couldn't conceive of Min holding a grudge against Ted, but some people did hold grudges.

"Did you know about this?" I demanded, striding toward the three of them.

The twins began to deny too loudly, but Ruby objected at just the right volume for someone who'd just come in and had no idea what was going on.

"Min Park." I told them, "He's back in town, and he's under arrest—or under interrogation, whatever—for burning down the Brew-Ha-Ha."

"That's ridiculous," Ruby said. Her manners always came off as just a touch too deliberate. She had a wide-eyed, expressive face and coquettish mannerisms that showed up in tiny ways: the way she walked, the way she flipped her hair. She had always gotten on my nerves. "I mean, you're like his best friend." Oh, and her presumptuous blanket statements.

"And your brother," I told Ruby, "was Min's worst bully. You'd think after fifteen years, Reuben would have given up on it and moved on, but if the first thing he does—"

Nadia got between us, saying, "Now hold on a minute—"

"—is call the cops on Min for some trumped-up charge. If he's still got Min in his crosshairs as if we all haven't grown the hell up—"

"I saw him!" Cody exclaimed, as if he'd been saying it in his own soft voice the whole time I was railing at Ruby. "I was at the Brew-Ha-Ha before the fire. I saw him. I told Detective Samberg yesterday."

I turned to Cody and tried to calm down. He was just a kid, after all. "How did you know it was Min Park?"

Cody twisted his fingers together nervously. "I didn't know. I just said who I saw: this tall Asian man in a three-piece suit and classy shoes.

It didn't look like someone who'd caused an accident. It looked like he knew what he was doing."

I didn't want to call Cody a liar, but my tone might have been on the sarcastic, incredulous side. "What were you doing up and about at that time?"

"I was coming back from the lake."

"And why were you at the lake?"

"I was doing some research on glow-in-the-dark jellyfish and algae." Without my asking, Cody supplied, "Not for school. I just like it, even though I knew I had work today."

Glow-in-the-dark jellyfish and algae? I was sure that Ontario wasn't the climate for those things, even if they did exist, but I'd have to ask Bea later on.

Naomi hummed in the way she did when she wanted to call attention to herself without people realizing. "I was at the Parks' grocery store that morning, and Mrs. Park was saying something about heading over to the Brew-Ha-Ha to talk sense into her son." She flinched when I glowered at her. "I told Detective Samberg that yesterday, too. He asked who could have been there so early, and I answered! I'm sorry, I thought you already knew he was in town."

Ruby cleared her throat. "Can we get back to the part where you chewed me out for something my brother did? I am really not involved with his life anymore."

"Or any of her family," Nadia added, taking Ruby's hand.

"Not that that's any of your business," Ruby added primly. "You shouldn't just jump to conclusions and yell at people, Cath."

I felt like a jerk all of a sudden. "I'm sorry. It's been a really awful couple of days, and—that's no excuse, I'm sorry. It's just that nobody's telling me anything."

Ruby seemed to accept my apology. "After the stuff's been filed for Naomi's car, why don't you come with us for lunch? It doesn't have as many kinds of tea and coffee as the Brew-Ha-Ha, but there's the Night Owl café—you know, part of the Night Owl bookstore? And their shepherd's pie is pretty good."

"Thanks," I told them, "but that sounds more like Bea's thing, and she's taken my aunt's cat to the vet, where I'm supposed to meet her after this. Maybe next time?"

"Just call us when things settle down," Naomi said.

When I left the town square, the sun was still out. I pulled out my cell and called Bea.

"Mission accomplished," I droned. "How's Marshmallow?"

Bea answered, "I looked into healing her, but it just looked bad enough that I wasn't even going to try, so the vet just put her on a drip and started a round of antibiotics. Maybe all the stress yesterday lowered her natural immunity or something. She's an old cat."

"Guess who I ran into?"

"Oh! Umm, uh… Min Park!"

I was startled. How did everybody else know these things? "How did you know that he was back?"

"Internet. You should really get on a social network, Cath—any social network. Any at all."

"Well," I said, feeling in my pocket for the chain and triangular pendant. Most of the soot had rubbed off, showing symbols on the faces of the pendant. I rubbed my fingers along the chain to shine it even more. "Some welcome-home he got—Detective Samberg was at the insurance office, and he told me that Min's being taken in for interrogation."

Her first response was low, loud, and long with Bea's disbelief. "No!" The next was a chirrup. "Seriously?"

"I've got to go over there," I told Bea. "Would you check in on your mother for me after you're done at the vet's?"

"Of course I will."

"Great. I'm going to get to the bottom of this." I ended the call and stood up, then I sat right back down. Bea could explain better the connection among the physical, the mental, and the magical when it comes to health. Magic burnout had left me feeling dizzy if I moved too fast.

Sometimes those old feelings of being orphaned just come up again and overtake me. I don't even realize it, so I just take for granted that I have to go some things alone.

I thought I was going to be the one to solve this mystery. I thought, with my best childhood friend as the prime suspect, that I had to be the only one. I was swallowing my anxiety over the possibility that I really didn't have what it took.

I've walked a delicate balance all my life, and in two days, that tightrope had snapped over the edge of a waterfall. I thought I had to fix this.

Sometimes I forgot that I did have a family and that, with them, I'm never really alone.

9. Scratching Post

Peanut Butter doesn't do well alone. When he's alone, sometimes he tries to talk to me in his head and tell me what he's up to. He can get needy and lonely. It's a good thing, really, that Treacle always finds ways into Bea's place that the feral cats in the neighborhood can't manage. Treacle might only keep doing that because he considers Peanut Butter a lot of fun to mess with, but he's never gone too far with his teasing. Besides, Peanut Butter appreciates the company.

That day, Treacle stayed with Peanut Butter even though he would rather have been somewhere else. That wasn't usual for Treacle since he was a wanderer. Peanut Butter was content just to have Treacle around until Peanut

Butter heard the scratchy popping of Treacle's cat claws against the carpet.

If they'd been humans, I could imagine this scene playing out with Treacle striking a punching bag with more grim determination than an ordinary fitness regimen would warrant—with the punching bag being a waterbed or something else breakable.

"Hey, hey—don't do that!" Peanut Butter told Treacle with a plaintive meow. The rest of the message would have been mind to mind: *"Mommy and Daddy don't like it. They only let me do it because I have blunters on my claws, and you don't even have those."*

Treacle replied, *"Good thing your mommy and daddy aren't here to stop me, then."*

Peanut Butter began to puff up his fur with fright. *"They're going to think your scratches are my fault, and they'll throw me out!"*

"You just said that you have nail blunters, so it couldn't be you. Go take a catnap."

"No! You stop that right now! Just stop it!"

"You can't make me." That wasn't a challenge but simply a statement of fact.

Well, it was a statement of what Treacle thought was a fact, anyway.

So Peanut Butter mauled Treacle.

Jake wasn't much of an animal lover at all, let alone a cat person. He wasn't allergic or, necessarily, cruel to animals—he'd just gathered that removing a cat's claws was a normal and sensible surgical procedure. He thought it was equivalent to neutering, without knowing, of course, that our cats couldn't care less about never getting to be fathers.

The declawing issue had been Jake and Bea's first really big fight, and with Peanut Butter's placid personality, all the arguments against declawing didn't apply as much. Peanut Butter was neither a hunter nor a fighter and was even willing to give up his claws to stop the arguing, but Astrid and Bea worried about muscular atrophy among other side effects, and the procedure would be something they couldn't undo. Preventing scratches on the furniture wasn't worth the risk of ruining the life of a living creature.

Jake had tried to get Peanut Butter to use a scratching post, and Peanut Butter did his own best to use the scratching post, but he wasn't always aware of when he started scratching at something because he did it out of anxiety most of the time.

I discovered nail caps for cats made out of vinyl, which stuck on with a nontoxic adhesive. Bea used them instead, and everybody was happy. Those were the nail blunters Peanut Butter was talking about.

For a timid kitty with nail blunters, Peanut Butter had quite the bite. He was no match for Treacle, who'd had a lifetime of street fighting the feral cats, but the attack came as a surprise to both of them.

Treacle's claw caught Peanut Butter's ear, enough to scrape the fur but not to draw blood. When Peanut Butter flattened his ears and gave a low, dangerous *mrrowl*, Treacle batted at Peanut Butter's head with a sheathed paw.

Treacle hissed. *"What's gotten into you?"*

Peanut Butter returned to his insecure anxiety for a moment but then steeled himself. *"You tell me. What's gotten into everybody? Is Marshmallow dying?"*

Treacle quickly hid his alarm. *"No. Marshmallow is just old and tired from doing magic."*

"Why would Marshmallow do so much magic?"

"I don't know! Because Marshmallow can do magic? We live with special humans. Magic is a part of life, and you and I will grow into it."

"I believe that's true"—Peanut Butter leapt onto the sofa and padded over to the window—*"but there's still something you're not telling me."*

Treacle leapt up to Peanut Butter and unnecessarily batted at his head again. *"Of course we never tell you anything! You're more prone to dying of fright than a rabbit!"*

"Ow! Stop it!" Peanut Butter leaped back a bit then licked his paw to clean his face. *"Are any of us going to die in some other way?"*

Treacle thought about it. *"I don't know. It's important that we all stay safe."*

Peanut Butter took that much better than Treacle expected. *"I want to know what's trying to hurt us."* Then he added, *"I'll fight to protect my family if I have to."*

"So would I," Treacle told him. *"But this is for our humans to find out. The best way that we can help them is to stay out of trouble."*

"You never stay out of trouble," Peanut Butter grumbled.

Treacle looked out the window and perked his ears up. *"You know what, P.B.? You're right. The best way to help would be to stay out of trouble…"* He bounded over to the cat door. *"It's not the only way to help, though!"*

"Wait for me!" Peanut Butter followed.

Outside, Treacle regarded Peanut Butter with apprehension. *"We need to go to the place where the bad thing happened. We have sharper eyes and better ears than humans. Maybe we can know something that they don't know."*

"Then I'll come with you. Two more eyes and ears should be twice as good!"

Treacle still didn't move. *"I might ask the street cats. They'll test us both harshly."*

"I'm a fast runner." That was a brave statement, coming from Peanut Butter.

"Stay away from the cars," Treacle advised before heading out.

10. A Doomed History

M eanwhile, Marshmallow and Bea returned to the old Greenstone house and spent the rest of the day there with Aunt Astrid. Marshmallow was still on her drip, in a cage, but she was feeling well enough by then to listen. That's how I know what went on that afternoon.

Aunt Astrid had been too exhausted to make herself a real breakfast, so Bea called to have a pizza and two liters of soda delivered and then basically threw together everything she could find in Astrid's pantry. Her resulting dish was a sort of rigatoni chicken stewed in white gravy, mushrooms, and parboiled root vegetables.

Aunt Astrid finished off the whole pizza by herself and still had room for a couple of bowls of what could be called Bea's accidental chowder.

Bea helped herself to a bowl while flipping through the spell book.

"For someone who loves books so much, you put them at risk a lot," Astrid warned from the soft armchair in which she rested. "That's one of a kind, bound by hand by Imogen Greenstone more than five hundred years ago. Every word in it brims with arcane power, and oh, the disaster that a single grease spot could cause—"

"All right, all right! I'm putting the soup away now, Mom." Bea set the bowl aside and smiled sincerely at her mother. "I'm glad that you have the energy to lecture me again."

She continued to flip through the supple vellum pages, reading the unfaded ink. It didn't feel like a magic book.

Whoever had written the Greenstone spell book took extra care to tie magic walls to the cover and pages. The spells would be powerful enough to break through the walls if they were read aloud or performed, but just reading them silently as Bea was doing wouldn't release anything too dangerous.

Bea read on with growing incredulity. Finally, she couldn't take it anymore. "These spells can't be real. Bringing the dead back to the prime of their life, using only a pound of bone from the deceased? Growing back all of the bones and the organs and the muscles, after which the resurrected would have eternal youth?"

"Keep reading."

Bea did. "Huh. This ritual required a coven of thirteen, and it sounds to me as if magic burnout took the lives of twelve of them—even though they took every precaution over the course of the nine months required to bring the subject back to life."

Astrid hummed an affirmative through a mouthful of chowder, swallowed, and chased it with a gulp of soda. "That's two of the reasons why we couldn't do that to Ted."

Bea flipped the page over again and found the other reason, written in a version of English older than standardized spelling. When Bea deciphered it, she balked. "They made a zombie! A violent undead cannibal!" She slammed the book shut and jumped back from it as if it were about to explode.

Aunt Astrid was unfazed. "Don't be afraid of the book itself, Bea. You know what they say. Those who don't learn from history are doomed to repeat it."

Bea objected, "When that doomed history is written out like a how-to manual, then it's more like those who do learn from history could have that problem! This is dark stuff, Mom. If it's at risk of falling into the wrong hands, we should destroy it—shouldn't we? It's not as if there's anything useful in there, anyway. It's all stuff that can cause fatal magic burnout and not one remedy for actual magic burnout! Not one!"

"No, no, no." Aunt Astrid beckoned her daughter. She took Bea's hands in hers and added seriously, "There are some good spells in there—if they aren't used the wrong way—and there are some blank pages, still. Those dark spells were written for a dark age, but you're an intelligent and kind young woman. You're a healer, too. You could be the one to add that magic burnout reversal spell, one day, to that book."

Bea shook her head. "I could never!"

Aunt Astrid peered at her in that amused sort of way that the wise gaze at smart alecks. "Only those who have lived forever and know the meaning of the word 'never' should be allowed to say it. Listen, Bea… Magic will always be around, lurking at the edges of the known world. It will always be powerful, but the question is whether it will also be wild. The book answers that question with, 'No, not if anybody in the Greenstone family can help it!' That's why we must keep it. When there's a disease, there's also an antidote. And what are the antidotes made out of? Disease. We need to know everything there is to know about magic so we can fight the bad part. This book is our antidote."

Someone knocked on their door.

"That might not be Cath," Bea said, taking the book and handing it to Astrid. "We need to keep this hidden."

"In plain sight," Astrid said. "You know my style."

"If it's Jake, remember that he likes books as much as I do. Also, he doesn't read silently."

"Oh. Right." Aunt Astrid shifted to hide the book under her seat cushion.

The caution was warranted, too, because Jake was indeed at the door. Bea greeted him warmly and asked about the investigation. He said he'd bring them up to speed, but first he asked after Aunt Astrid's health.

"Low blood pressure," Aunt Astrid lied. "It gets worse with age, but it's nothing serious."

Bea offered him a lunch of accidental chowder. "Sorry, sweetheart, you missed the pizza." She quickly finished her own bowl of chowder. "And I miss Ted already. He knew how to make a potage."

Even the simplest dish of his would have a dash of an herb or spice to make it something more than ordinary.

"The whole town will miss him," Jake said. "Anybody who'd ever been to the Brew-Ha-Ha, anyway. Darla Castellan was inconsolable."

"Histrionics," Aunt Astrid said dismissively. "That little tart."

"Oh, Jake wouldn't fall for that! Would you, sweetheart?"

Jake shrugged. "She might have been inconsolable for the wrong reasons, but I'd say that it was honest grief. You can't string along a dead man."

Bea blinked, processing that. "Darla… stringing along… Ted?"

Jake sat down with his bowl of chicken chowder. "Yeah. Apparently, they were dating— off and on. She must have preferred that kind of melodrama." He ate a spoonful. "This isn't bad." He caught the flabbergasted expressions on Astrid and Bea's faces. "He never talked about his life outside of work, then? I was hoping that one of you could confirm or discredit something I learned from Miss Castellan about Ted's troubled family history."

Aunt Astrid's eyes had widened in disbelief. "No," she said. "He never mentioned any of this to us. And Darla—that's a surprise."

"He must have known that Cath would never let him hear the end of it," Bea remarked. "Darla was so mean to Cath in school."

"I guess his good taste stayed literal," Jake said. At that moment, Bea's cell phone rang. Jake checked the number on the screen for her. "It's Nadia LaChance."

He handed the phone over to Bea, who answered with, "Hey, girl!"

"Please control your sister."

"Sis… You mean Cath? Is that what this is about?"

"Yeah. Cousin. Whatever! I hate her so much today. Do you know that she started yelling at Ruby for no reason, and my useless sister apologized to her? Ruby even invited her to lunch!"

Bea flinched. "I hate to break it to you, Nadia, but there's nothing to be done about Cath when she's on a mission. And this time, it's actually important."

Nadia swore and hung up.

Aunt Astrid groaned. "Cath wouldn't. Not in her"—she glanced at Jake and lowered her voice—"condition."

"Blood pressure issues run in the family," Bea told Jake, which wasn't a lie but wasn't an explanation either.

Jake accepted it anyway. "I'd rather Cath not interfere with the investigation, of course. Samberg will slap the cuffs on some poor kid for jaywalking—you know how I've been complaining about that—but when it's serious like this, he could be the best person on the case. If he could keep his mind on the case, that is." Jake smiled in something between amusement and veiled chagrin.

Bea read the expression instantly. "You think that Detective Samberg has a crush on Cath? They only just met yesterday!"

"Oh, no, not a crush. Samberg went to follow the money." Jake tried to gloss over the crush business. "Insurance fraud attempt took an unfortunate turn for the homicidal—that was Samberg's theory. That's how he thinks. I know it's ridiculous. He tells me that my personal life compromises my investigation skills, and we part ways. I have to say, if we had more detectives in this town, I wouldn't be working on this case, but I have to since Samberg is the only other detective now that Bill went to Montreal. He's new, and he'd mess up without me."

Aunt Astrid and Bea murmured their encouragement.

Jake held a hand up for silence, maybe partly out of humility but mostly out of excitement. "But Cath? She knocked him off that trail in under a minute. Samberg can only be head over heels in love with her."

Aunt Astrid gave a long, drawn-out "Ohhh..." the way mothers do when the young women they've always taken care of find someone special. She was probably imagining us walking down the aisle.

Bea waved her hands in refusal, almost laughing. "Enough! Enough, please, no more relationship gossip! Tell us about Ted's family."

"I don't know how much I'm allowed to tell. It's only Miss Castellan's statement, but..." Jake sighed. "Ted Lanier might have gotten caught up in some organized crime syndicate and run up some debts, and maybe they took it out on his son."

"Is that why Min Park is your prime suspect?" Bea asked. "He's Asian, so he must be a member of the yakuza? That's so racist!"

"My wife is psychic," Jake remarked.

"No!" Bea's voice pitched high with momentary panic. "Cath called me while I was at the vet's, that's all. She'd heard from Detective Samberg that Min was being held there."

"Interrogated," Jake corrected, "not jailed. We've found no connection between Min Park and organized crime. None at all. We only have witnesses that put him near the Brew-Ha-Ha at the time of the fire."

Aunt Astrid objected, "The Parks have always been upstanding members of our community. Mrs. Park was the first person to check in on us when the fire brigade came."

"Was she?" Jake's voice sharpened.

An awkward silence ensued before Aunt Astrid answered, "Yes."

"That's interesting." Jake set his bowl down. He'd had only a couple spoonfuls. Distractedly, he said, "Well, that was delicious, but I've got to get back to work now."

"Jake, wait!" Bea said. "I have to tell you something."

Aunt Astrid kept silent.

Bea went over to embrace her husband. "Please stay safe," she begged, her voice muffled against his shoulder. "Don't get shot. Don't get held hostage in a warehouse somewhere by gangsters in suits. Please come back home safe to me."

"Of course I will. I promise." Jake returned her embrace. After a moment, he wondered aloud, "Would this thing that you're doing be equally convincing to Cath?"

"Nope," Bea answered accurately. She pulled away, more cavalier. "Cath's a force of nature. You've just got to deal with her as she comes. Good luck!"

They both said, "I love you," and then Jake left. Bea saw him out the front door.

When she returned, Aunt Astrid breathed a sigh of relief. "You really had me going for a moment there, Kitten. I thought you were finally going to tell him about our family secret."

"This is so wrong." Bea hugged herself and ambled to the window to watch Jake cross the street. "We can't throw the Parks under the bus, ruin their lives, and frame innocent people just so that we can keep our secret! Maybe if Jake knew, he could solve the case for real and make a cover story for us."

"Maybe," Aunt Astrid allowed. "Maybe not. Would you be so cruel as to burden him with the same double life as ours, and him without any magical talents?"

"I just wish I could do something."

At that, Aunt Astrid suggested, "Act normal. Call the LaChance girl, make amends, and go out with your friends tonight. Tell them about my low blood pressure and Cath's worrying penchant for vigilante justice." When Bea looked doubtful, Aunt Astrid added, "That will help us all more than you know. I'll be here with Marshmallow. Do you really want to be running around and yelling at people with Cath? How much of a good cop can you really be?"

11. Joy Ride

I didn't know any of this was going on as I headed toward the police station. Out of the corner of my eye, a black car slunk up beside the sidewalk with the passenger's window down. Blake Samberg peered at me and waved from the driver's seat. The car slowed to a stop as I approached and stuck my head in the window.

"So," I asked him, "Am I breaking some speed limit for pedestrians? Are you going to write me a ticket?"

"No," he answered. He really didn't have a sense of humor. "You're on the way to the station. Let me drive you."

"You know how townsfolk talk. I wouldn't want them to get the wrong idea, to see me picked up in a squad car." I silently noted that the vehicle was unmarked. I hadn't even known the Wonder Falls Police Department had cars like that.

"Nobody we take in for an interrogation rides up front."

I raised an eyebrow, mulling over how shady the entire situation could be.

Blake continued, "Besides, the way you were hollering back at the office? It sounds to me as if you can take care of yourself."

"You're not swinging by for Jake, then?"

"Jake?"

I stared at him before carefully enunciating, "Detective Williams."

At that, Blake gave the slightest of flinches and shook his head.

"What happened? Would your chief even let you just split up like that?"

Blake looked at me gravely. He looked serious all the time, from what I knew of him, but his darkness deepened. "I'll tell you on the way."

With my magic burnout, could I really take care of myself against Blake? But why assume the worst? I didn't know enough about anything yet. I'd only suggested that Blake had done it because I hadn't liked him when I'd first met him, which had been one day earlier.

I got into the car.

"Would you say that honesty with partners is important?" Blake asked as he turned down the sunny main street.

I looked at him sidelong. "Is this a date?"

"Williams thinks that I stick to the rules too much when I call him out." Blake gritted his teeth at the injustice of it. "He's too close to this case to be objective."

"Because of Bea?" Even though I knew Blake was angry—and even taking into consideration both my having just met him and his being in the driver's seat—I couldn't let that stand. "Oh, please! Have you met Jake Williams? Have you seen Jake Williams meet anybody else? He's close to everybody in this town. He's such a nice guy that everyone tells him everything. They can't help it."

"That didn't happen with me. When I told Jake everything that was on my mind, he went off alone and told me not to go near him. Let him explain that to the chief!"

"Stop the car right now!"

He didn't brake with a jolt, but he reluctantly slowed down and warily looked at me. No, not at me—past me.

The reason I'd told him to stop was that he'd been so busy ranting that he hadn't seen Cody about to cross the street. Now Blake eyed the poor kid the way Treacle eyes a mouse. Treacle, unlike many other cats, does not play with his food.

"This isn't a crossing area," Blake murmured.

I saw him moving to pounce and pulled him back by his jacket. "We're investigating a murder!" I snapped. "It doesn't count as jaywalking when everybody knows cutting across Main Street here is the fastest route to the grocery from the town square."

I was sure that would be wrong in Blake's book, but every driver in Wonder Falls knew it. Somehow, setting up the crossing lights and painting the pedestrian lane just kept getting passed over in the beautification society's itinerary.

Then Blake did something unexpected. He smiled, just for a moment. "You said we're investigating a murder. We."

"Separately." I was not disarmed by his smile. "I wouldn't want to interfere with the official investigation, but I can't sit back and do nothing." I added, warning him, "I'm not nearly as objective as Jake."

Blake nodded and drove on. "You know, I thought you'd stopped me there because you'd had enough of me after two seconds and wanted out, as if you'd rather walk the rest of the way. I'm glad that wasn't the case."

"I can see your elation."

I didn't mean to pick on him. The idea that Jake was nice to absolutely everybody in town except for Blake must have stung enough.

"As civil servants, Williams and I have got limitations that a citizen such as yourself wouldn't have. I wouldn't get in your way, either. But I'd like to be in the know."

"Oh, would you?"

"Jake plays nice. You're not afraid to speak your mind," Blake said. "I know this case is personal to you, and that's why you won't stop until you've found the truth. That's why I need you. I couldn't admit to being a confidant, though."

"Or an informant!"

"Do we have a deal, then?"

"None that either of us could admit to," I said.

We'd arrived at the police station.

Blake got out of the car first, came around to my side, and opened the door for me. He muttered, "Williams thinks that I stick to the rules. He's wrong."

"Yeah. Real renegade, you are, letting that jaywalker go." I hesitated, but if I wanted him to think we were working together—and that I was getting anywhere—then I had to give him something. "I stole evidence from the crime scene."

Blake looked stunned then glanced around to make sure no one was listening.

I continued, "I'm sure that it belonged to the murderer, but I'm not sure if the murderer noticed that it was gone. If I show it to Min Park and he doesn't recognize it, then that would prove that he's innocent."

"Or it would implicate him, say, if he does know that he lost this piece of evidence and would deny anything that would tie him to the crime."

"That would still be something." Part of me was convinced Min wouldn't know what the necklace was, and he would be honest about that, too.

Blake nodded curtly. "Let me see what you took."

I shook my head. "Let me see Min."

I wanted to see Blake's reaction, too, when the pyramid necklace came out. I would have to be quick.

12. Lost and Found

The police station was entirely open, with no cubicle walls or even offices, only an empty holding cell in one corner. I saw the interrogation room with the one-way mirror, where I hoped Min was.

Blake told me to wait on a bench by the cooler while the police chief, old Talbot, took him aside for a talk. Blake explained that he and Jake still kept each other up to speed on important information despite having parted ways for the investigation. The police chief was more concerned about why they'd parted ways in the first place.

A third man emerged from the hall and approached them, and the police chief greeted him with respectful formality as "Mr. Park."

I barely recognized him, and not just because of the suit, the haircut, the pimple-free complexion, and the fancy shoes. The Min Park I'd known had a habit of hunching his shoulders protectively. He stammered everything he said as if he were breaking the worst of news to the listener.

Whoever this man was looked dismayed, even embarrassed—who wouldn't be when taken in for an interrogation?—but he had a serenity about him that comes only from being comfortable in one's own skin. His hair was gelled back neatly, and his eyes were warm.

I approached them cautiously, hardly believing my eyes.

Min recognized me instantly and shouted, "Cath! Cath!" Laughing, he pulled me in for a big hug.

Even though he'd never done that before, something about the way he did it reassured me that my old friend was still in there. The best way I can describe it was that Min was like a puppy. Min used to be a sad puppy, but he turned into a happy one.

I couldn't help laughing, too. "I didn't know that you were in town!"

"I wanted it to be a surprise." He looked around. "Not this kind of surprise."

"You are the silver lining in the nightmare storm cloud that the past two days have been," I reassured him. I turned to Blake and Chief Talbot. "Are we all done here?"

Chief Talbot kept a suspicious eye on Blake as he answered, "We wouldn't dream of keeping you, Miss Greenstone."

And Blake, keeping a steely look on me, answered, "Keep in touch, Cath."

Min looked at Blake, startled, and couldn't disguise his renewed dismay. I used the opportunity to drop the pyramid necklace behind me as I took a step back.

"Cath," Min began, pointing at Blake, "is this—?"

"He's Jake's partner. You know Jake Williams?"

"Bea's husband." Min nodded.

"Jake and Blake are both working on the case with the fire at the Brew-Ha-Ha," I answered, hooking Min's arm in mine. "I'll show you around town for the rest of the day. It's been a long time. You'll be surprised at how little has changed."

I stepped on the necklace chain and pretended to slip a little. "Oh!" I said, leaning down and picking it up. "This must be yours. It must have fallen when you tackled me." I straightened up and dangled the pyramid pendant in front of us, looking sidelong at Blake.

He was good at not changing his expression, but I could see that the blood had drained from his face. Blake, the hardboiled criminal detective, recognized the pendant as I held it up—and it scared him.

Caught you, I thought grimly.

Min said, "Huh, I thought I lost that. Thanks."

I turned my head toward him. "Wait, what?" The necklace dropped from my fingers in my shock. Min already had his hand stretched out to catch it. He wrapped the chain over his index and middle fingers and stuffed the bundle into his breast pocket.

He extended his arm gracefully. "Shall we?"

I mustered up some courtesy and took his arm. "So we shall! Why do you have a four-sided-die necklace and keep it in your breast pocket?"

"Oh, I joined a club—kind of," Min told me. "It was boring. I don't miss anyone, and they didn't deliver on anything that they promised. But they gave that away as part of their new membership packet, and I think it looks kind of cool, so I kept it. It never matches with anything I usually wear now, though."

I still had a bit of magic burnout, but if Min had had a memory spell cast on him, or if what happened was magical in any way, I'd still feel it.

13. Hide and Seek

Meanwhile, Treacle and Peanut Butter had found their way to the crime scene. Treacle hadn't been to the Brew-Ha-Ha since he was a kitten. Ted hadn't allowed it after that first time, which Treacle remembered well.

Ted had claimed banning Treacle was for hygiene reasons. I'd argued that Marshmallow came into the café and even the kitchen all the time, but Ted had argued that Marshmallow would stay put, whereas street cats went all over the place and you couldn't stop them.

I'd almost argued that Marshmallow's hair got all over the place and nobody minded, or that maybe Ted had allowed Marshmallow because he thought Aunt Astrid had more clout than I did.

Really, Ted was afraid of black cats and particularly afraid of crossing their paths. I'd noticed he wasn't interested at all in Aunt Astrid's fortunetelling, either. Maybe a black cat with a star on his forehead was too ominously witchy.

Treacle had kept out of the way since telling me Ted's fear, or else he waited out front. The town had more interesting places for a cat to explore, anyway.

Aunt Astrid had been right. Ted wasn't interested because of a belief in magic. If he had been outright opposed to it, then he first would have stolen and destroyed Aunt Astrid's completely nonmagical tarot cards and slightly magical crystal balls. If he'd found the secret trapdoor into Aunt Astrid's nuclear war bunker, Ted would probably have ignored the book and used the space to store wines or something.

But that was all over, and the cats were at the Brew-Ha-Ha. Treacle hadn't been there in a long while, as I mentioned, and Peanut Butter had never been.

The place was also crowded with investigators.

Jake had dropped in to check on what his colleagues had turned up so far. The kitchen still had the yellow crime-scene tape cordoning off the area, and it was more crowded than it should have been because all the bagging of possible evidence and photographing of the scene should have been done the day before.

"I'd hate to say it," began Jason Boone, who was in charge of cataloguing, "but we're in over our heads with this. We could use someone more practiced, you know, dealing with cases like this."

Jake knew what he was talking about. "Blake Samberg's made up his own mind about what happened, and I'm letting him investigate that. Let's just do our best to get the evidence in."

Boone sighed. "Those damn strays." He waved a rubber-gloved hand toward Treacle and Peanut Butter, who were slinking in from what used to be the restaurant area.

Jake turned to look. "Those aren't strays!" He was surprised to see Peanut Butter out. He jogged toward them, as if skittish cats would keep still in a strange place—even being approached by somebody they knew. "Get back here, Peanut Butter! And you!"

"Leave it to Williams!" Boone called out to one of the investigators, who still wore their protective overalls, paper shoes, face masks, and white rubber gloves. "Don't contaminate the evidence!"

Peanut Butter hid in a corner. Treacle ran behind the bar, where the trapdoor was. Jake stopped at the door, realizing the cats would run if he kept going after them.

He crouched down in front of Treacle. "All right, come on… come on, kitty."

Peanut Butter calmed down a bit and came up to Jake, rubbing his head against Jake's knee and meowing.

"See? Peanut Butter's fine here with me." He picked up Peanut Butter in one hand, reached out to slowly and gently catch Treacle in the same way, lost his balance, and slipped. Treacle dodged the falling Jake as Peanut Butter leapt from Jake's grasp.

Boone poked his head into the room. "Are the cats giving you any trouble there, Williams?"

"No," Jake said gruffly.

Peanut Butter bounded over behind Treacle, who was licking his own paw. Jake pressed against the floor to push himself up, and the latch nudged ever so slightly, telling him he wasn't pressing on solid floor.

"No," Jake repeated quietly as he pushed himself up. "They're not giving any trouble at all." He found the handle, disguised as a missing floor tile, and pulled the trapdoor up.

Treacle, seeing the opportunity, bolted into the opening.

"Boone," Jake ordered, "get the rest of the team in here."

Jason looked at him blankly. "For a cat?"

"For an investigation! If Astrid Greenstone knew about this, then she forgot. Maybe the perpetrator didn't."

The only clue they found was a shoe print. They, like Aunt Astrid and me, didn't have Treacle's sharp feline senses.

14. To Catch a Fish

I wish I could say that I enjoyed that afternoon, spending time with Min Park after a decade apart. In all the ways that mattered, we'd stayed the same, still best friends. The stuff with Ted and the spell book had thrown me for a bad turn, though.

We dropped by the Parks' grocery store, and I saw the new Min Park rubbing off on his family.

Mrs. Park's wrinkled face beamed with joy as she loudly declared what an accomplishment her son was.

"My husband is a manager. He doesn't own this business, you know."

"I know." I'd known that since I was young, but I still thought Mr. Park had a decent job.

"Min owned his tech company. He sold it! He is… how do you say… set for life!"

Min gave an embarrassed laugh. "Let's not be too loud about that, Mom."

A lot of things had changed since our childhood. Being wealthy wasn't just a pipe dream anymore. A memory nudged at me, of Min and I wondering what we would do if money were no object. "I guess you can have that UFO built, huh?"

"I can say, with my degree in engineering, that this is completely possible. Give science just another three years to advance, and I'll bet sound waves and cymatics will bring us closer to a functioning tractor beam than magnetic force." Min tapped his chin thoughtfully. "We won't get to go into outer space, though—at least, not with the windshield-like clear panel—because of the radiation. Besides, we'd need to travel faster than light to get anywhere interesting. I'd rather invest in terraforming a planet."

"But it would look just like earth! There'd be no point!" I exclaimed with a laugh. We'd both known that since we were kids. It was part of the running joke.

"Seriously, though." Min Park put an arm around his mother. "I think it's time that I settled down and started taking care of my parents in their old age."

Mrs. Park hugged him back. "My son is ridiculous. So thoughtful! But no. That's your money. Your father and I love to manage this shop. We love this town."

Mrs. Park had the same warmth and reassuring presence as Aunt Astrid. Mr. Park tended to be steelier. He and Min weren't getting along by the time Min was in his teens. I'd always been intimidated by Mr. Park.

So that's why, when Min excused himself to go talk with his father, we both understood that would be a private conversation.

I needed to hold my own conversation with Mrs. Park.

"You could have mentioned that Min was back," I said to her.

"I am sorry." She did look sorry. Her voice became quiet again. It wasn't a whisper, but I had to lean close to listen. "I had my reasons. Please don't make me repeat them. Jake Williams has already interrogated my whole family."

I said to her, "If you won't tell your side, Mrs. Park, then other townspeople are going to. I heard one witness say that you wanted to talk sense into your son. Why didn't he have any sense in him already?"

Mrs. Park sighed.

"He was at the Brew-Ha-Ha before it caught fire, and you knew. Don't let me keep thinking the worst, Mrs. Park." I said sincerely, "Please."

"All right," Mrs. Park said. "Min hates this town. After he sold the business, he traveled all over the world, looking for nice towns and cities, sending Mr. Park and me postcards saying that we should move there with him. Mr. Park refused him, told him to quit showing off."

"Well, that's harsh. Did Min come back as a final act of persuasion?" I asked, looking across the grocery aisle at Min and his father. They were shaking hands.

"No. He knows his father too well." At last, Mrs. Park mustered up some strength behind her voice. "Still, he came back to this hometown of his, from his travels so far away. He couldn't sleep. What do you call it? Plane…"

I thought for a moment. "Jet lag?"

"Yes. Thank you. He wanted to go out for a walk. When the other detective came to arrest him, he said the whole thing was suspicious."

"Blake said so? Detective Samberg?"

"The nerve of that man!"

"He's suspicious of everything and everyone, though."

"What about the witness—that teenage boy who said that Min started the fire? What was he doing? Studying the glow-in-the-dark plants and animals in the lake, in the woods, alone? I can't believe it, but he... that detective—" She cut herself off.

I thought about Cody. When Bea had been his age, she'd been more interested in experimentation and travel than just reading about scientific facts and foreign places. After graduating high school, Bea had planned and saved up to go backpacking around Antarctica, of all things. There's a fine line between genius and craziness, and I sensed the same attitude in Cody. "I believe both of you. It's complicated. Cody must have been mistaken."

Mrs. Park, uncharacteristically, reached out to take my hand. "Thank you. This is the best life we could have hoped for, Mr. Park and I. Still, it's so difficult in this town! The way people talk!"

I couldn't tell her how much I understood. Being a witch might have been a private subculture for generations, but you couldn't tell just by looking at us that we weren't like everyone else.

On the other hand, once nonwitches knew who was a witch... Let's just say history doesn't show that people have a good record of getting over and getting used to it so that witches could just be treated like people again.

At least Min had gotten the chance to shine, to change whatever people used to think about him.

"That's why," Mrs. Park told me, "I told him that I would rather he go find a nice Korean girl to settle down with."

I felt a brief twist of envy, which I tried to disguise as surprise. Min was a friend. Min was a good old friend. "If that's what Min wants, he shouldn't have any trouble! He's obviously a catch, Mrs. Park."

"It is difficult to catch a fish gone over the falls." Mrs. Park made no gesture to emphasize what she really meant, so figuring it out took me a while.

"So that's the real reason that you didn't tell me," I said to her. "You think Min likes me?"

Mrs. Park shook her head. "I don't think. A mother just knows these things."

"Min and I are friends," I said, as much to myself as to her. "We even need to get to know each other again. You've got the whole afternoon to see that we're just big kids, and it's just like before the fire. It's just like it was before this awful investigation started."

I wanted that to be true. I'd grown up with these people even if Mrs. Park didn't consider me an honorary family member. Everyone in every family has their… not secrets, not privacy, just boundaries. Expectations. The Parks didn't deserve the suspicion of other townspeople.

But I couldn't help harboring my own suspicions.

15. Respectable Accusers

At dusk, Bea called me on my cell. I could barely hear her over the background noise and electronic music.

"Bea, where are you?" I asked, standing on the grocery store's balcony. I guess it was meant for employees on their smoke breaks. It was empty and had a view of the town.

"I'm at the Night Owl. Decent book selection, terrible café. But that just might be today. Everybody who would be at the Brew-Ha-Ha came here instead. It used to be quiet enough to browse and do some reading."

"How's Aunt Astrid?"

"Well enough to shoo me outside for a night out with the girls."

The girls in question hollered their hellos.

I groaned, thinking about that morning. "Has Nadia forgiven me yet?"

"Nadia? I talked her out of reporting you to Detective Samberg for a hate crime, but I'll tell her that you're sorry—"

Nadia's voice rose above the background chatter to cuss me out: "Ruby's brother is a sore spot with her, you know. If you think he was unpleasant to you at school, imagine living with him."

"Let me go to the restroom where it's quieter," Bea said.

"He was so mean to Min at school," I said. "And Ruby's the best friend of the worst bully, Darla Castellan! The only friend, by now."

"With friends like Ruby, Darla doesn't need to antagonize anybody," Bea said.

The background noise became muffled. Bea must have found the restroom.

"Darla killed Ted for fun, then," I said.

"Oh, don't start! You know that I only have so much tolerance for mean, insipid gossip." Bea droned, "Clutch the pearls! Darla strung our Ted along, and that's why she didn't divorce until recently! Oh, my stars! Min Park's so handsome now—and a criminal! He's sexy now because he's dangerous! So much chatter in this town."

"No offense, Bea, but I thought your friends would have a better perspective after Naomi and Ruby got together."

"Apparently, if you can't beat 'em, then join 'em." Bea sighed. "The chef at the Night Owl is willing to stock our pastries once the Brew-Ha-Ha building is back up, by the way."

"That's great news."

"Now," Bea said, "you tell me something important."

I told her about a possible fraternity that marked its members with magical pendants.

"And Min was a member?" Bea asked. "You've got to bring him over here! We can ask him together! Discreetly, of course."

"With your friends treating him like an escaped felon when it was only an interrogation?"

"That'll show more people that it was only an interrogation. And an interrogation is just questions, like we'll ask him. Bookstore café, police department—just innocent, curious questions to find out the truth—"

At that moment, the balcony door swung open, and Min strode through, talking on his phone, sounding upset.

"No, today—tonight, whatever!" He paused. "I'm not going anywhere. You already know where my parents live and at which inn I booked a room. You should be the one to come to me for follow-up questions." He paused. "Fine." Then he hung up.

He told me, "This is just embarrassing. The chief wants me to meet with him for some follow-up questions. It's not as if they found new evidence in the past six hours."

"Ridiculous," I agreed, hanging up on Bea, knowing that she'd heard him. "I told Blake that you couldn't fight your way out of a wet paper bag. He probably wants to update that information since we aren't ten anymore." I laughed. "You know, I can't even remember that? What was it, a wet paper bag in a pool beside the gym?"

Min didn't laugh. "It was a burlap sack. Reuben Connors tied the sack shut, hauled me onto a boat, and pushed it downriver toward the falls. He called me 'pipsqueak.'"

I remembered then. Maybe I'd changed it to a paper bag because the reality was much more depressing.

I had chased after that boat, reached out with my mind for the Maid of the Mist, and begged her to do something. If she had had any part in it, I didn't see her, but I like to think that's when I awakened to my power. All the eels and fish and everything in the lake swarmed around to bump against the boat, pushing it away from the rapids and the falls. The boat found a riverbank instead, and I got Min Park out of the sack safely.

Maybe I'd thought it was a swimming pool because I confused myself with how Darla would steal my swimsuit or my clothes while we were swimming in phys ed class. The other girls in my grade, who tried to stay out of it, were probably even worse than the ones who laughed. I'd felt so alone.

All that had been a lifetime ago for me. Min's face, clouded over with an almost Blake-ish brooding, told me that—despite the wealth, the achievements, and all the new friends he'd met in foreign places—the horrors of his youth weren't over for Min. I felt terrible for him because I completely understood.

"Reuben wasn't just a bully," I realized. "He really liked to make people suffer, and it hasn't served him well in this town. He's a nothing, Min. He has no power over you."

"Right," Min said. I could tell he was forcing a smile. "We've all grown up. Every encounter since high school ended is out of my mind. Reuben who?"

"That's the spirit!"

"I won't let him ruin this comeback!"

"Atta boy!"

"However, getting taken into police custody for arson and murder isn't something that I'd 'let' ruin my day so much as it's kind of a day-ruiner as a point of fact."

"He did accuse you, then?" I wondered.

Min replied, "He threw a shoe at the police-car window when it passed him, and I was in it."

"That's not a statement the cops would find worth considering," I said confidently. "No one in this town would bend an ear to such a lowlife."

"And my more respectable accusers?"

"They'll be proven wrong," I said with a simple confidence I didn't feel. I'd used magic for Min. Maybe he'd remembered those strange happenings when I'd let some magic slip or forgot that he wasn't supposed to know.

Maybe he'd come back for revenge, but he knew we wouldn't use our magic to help him with that, so he somehow figured out we had a spell book and took it.

I wanted to ask about his father and hear something good about how their relationship would proceed. A growing part of me even wanted to have a moment with him on that balcony, watching the sunset. He seemed so innocent, and I wanted to fight for that innocence if it was true, against all the lies floating around town.

But the truth was that I didn't know him anymore.

I didn't know anything anymore.

So instead I said, "Do you want me to come with you to meet with Talbot?"

Min shook his head, still looking glum.

It was on the tip of my tongue to say, "Too bad, I'm coming with you anyway," but I was too confused and had no plan.

16. Gone

S o I went home. I took a detour to the falls to clear my head, though. I've seen enough photos and sunsets or sunrises over the falls to last a lifetime, but that time of day when drivers don't know whether to turn their headlights on or keep them off just washes everything in soft blues. It's nature's own magic.

Repeat

So I went home. I took a detour to the falls to clear my head, though. I've seen enough photos and sunsets or sunrises over the falls to last a lifetime, but that time of day when drivers don't know whether to turn on or leave off their headlights just washes the world in soft blues. It's nature's own magic.

I might have accidentally discovered a cure for magic burnout right then. I wonder if nonwitches just feel magic burnout all the time. The static crackle that had been distracting me

122

the whole day smoothed over until I felt more like myself again. My mind flowed out into the world and into all the connections I'd made—as it was meant to.

As my head cleared, an image entered my mind, of Aunt Astrid lying on the downstairs living-room carpet, and my body went cold with shock when I smelled blood through Peanut Butter's nose.

"Help! Oh, help!" Peanut Butter wailed in my mind. *"Treacle's gone, and Grandmommy won't move! I found her this way, and I didn't know what to do!"*

An image that felt more like one of Peanut Butter's memories appeared in my mind. He'd followed the smell of Bea's shoes to a loud place full of people—the Night Owl.

That was interrupted by an earlier memory— Min Park's formal shoes in an alleyway.

"I thought that Chief Talbot wanted to meet me," Min said. He must have been speaking to somebody.

"I said that to throw Miss Greenstone off our trail," answered a low, gravelly voice. "I really apologize for the inconvenience, Mr. Ark."

"It's Park."

"If things had gone differently, we would be calling one another 'brother.'"

"Mom!" Bea screamed in the present image. She fell to her knees beside Aunt Astrid's body. Sobbing, she checked for a pulse then for magic burn, and then she took about four deep breaths to calm herself. She needed a calm mind to do her healing.

The memory flowed back in. Peanut Butter was hiding in some old crate or box in the alleyway, knowing that Treacle was listening in from a nearby fire escape.

"I don't have any brothers."

"No. You don't claim to be part of the Order anymore, right?"

Treacle yowled as he fell to the ground. He landed on his feet, as cats do, and Blake swore and grabbed my cat.

"I didn't know what to do!" Peanut Butter wailed again. *"They went away together. They took Treacle with them!"*

I snapped out of it, reached for my phone, and dialed for an ambulance as I bolted home. The dispatcher kept asking me questions or giving me directions as if I were actually at the scene, which of course I wasn't. I could only see through Peanut Butter's eyes.

As soon as the dispatcher said the ambulance was on the way, I hung up and crossed Main Street into the town square. I didn't want the dispatcher to overhear the background noise of traffic and people milling about and realize I wasn't actually at home. Hiding these things had become second nature. I could only hope that was good enough because I might have been getting a reputation with the dispatcher.

The ambulance got there quickly, which was a minor relief, but I wasn't there with Bea and Astrid to know what was going on, which was a major anxiety.

When I arrived at the house, the door was closed and locked. I took the spare key from the flowerpot hanging on the trellis and went inside. I found Peanut Butter in the living room and Marshmallow still in her cage in Aunt Astrid's bedroom. All Marshmallow knew was that Aunt Astrid had gone to make herself dinner, and she'd taken the book with her.

Peanut Butter caught me up on Bea's cover story: she'd found Peanut Butter wandering around outside the Night Owl and decided to take him home. On the way, she met with me. We decided to go to Astrid's place instead, where we found her. I called the ambulance and went upstairs, out of sight of the paramedics. Bea had called Jake to pick me up.

With a little of Peanut Butter's help and a lot of Marshmallow's, we searched the house for the book. The old Greenstone house had a few loose floorboards that Aunt Astrid would hide things under, and Marshmallow knew them all. Peanut Butter and I searched them all.

I had no doubt about it. The real spell book was gone.

17. The Order

J ake and I were silent as he drove me to the hospital. I kept reaching out to Treacle in my mind, but something kept blocking me—until suddenly, the blockage wasn't there anymore.

"Is it safe to talk now? I thought there was magic— bad magic, from somebody else." Treacle spoke in my mind, but I couldn't see anything from him but pitch blackness.

Contrary to popular belief, cats can't see in complete darkness. Their eyes just function much better than most human eyes do at low light levels.

"Treacle," I murmured. *"What happened?"*

"I'm not hurt."

"But where are you?"

"I don't know. It doesn't smell familiar."

I felt a steel grid through Treacle's whiskers and smelled dye and fabric that had been used to cover the grid.

Treacle asked, *"Why couldn't I talk to you? Was it because of magic burnout? You seem fine now. More than fine!"*

"No," I told Treacle. *"Not magic burnout. Something else."*

Jake cleared his throat as he drove. "Funny thing. Treacle and Peanut Butter interfered with the crime scene today."

"I keep telling Treacle not to go wandering off!" I whispered, hating the tremor of terror and regret in my voice. Then I bit my tongue. "I mean, I do what I can. Locking the cat flap door and all that."

Jake gave me a doubtful look. "They helped us to find evidence."

"Really?"

Jake nodded his head toward the dashboard, where I saw some fully developed photographs of the inside of Aunt Astrid's bunker. I picked up one of a shoeprint. Through Peanut Butter's eyes, Blake had some nice shoes, too.

"I think these animals really do know what's going on sometimes," Jake said.

I told Jake, "That's more than me these past two days."

After the hospital workers rolled Astrid out of the emergency room, Bea slept sitting on a plastic chair by her mother's hospital bed. That would make it easier for Bea to use her talent.

I warned her about magic burnout, but she turned her despairing eyes to me and asked, "What use is my power if I can't save my own mother?"

I sat down on the armchair in the corner and didn't argue.

When she couldn't heal Astrid any more, Bea said, "I can't believe I didn't check for the book!"

"It was gone before you came in." That wasn't exactly reassuring.

"There were supposed to be protection spells in the Greenstone house. What happened?"

I said grimly, "The Order. They have magic."

"Min did this? Or Detective Samberg?"

"I don't know. Still, it's the Order that broke down the protection spells. Aunt Astrid's magic burnout was worse than mine. She and Marshmallow would both have been numb to the spells disintegrating." I massaged the sides of my head. "Something keeps stopping me from getting in touch with Treacle. It's either Min or Blake. They were meeting with each other while Aunt Astrid was being attacked. That much I do know."

Peanut Butter had bolted out of his hiding place in the alleyway the moment Min and Blake walked away. He'd gone to alert Marshmallow that Treacle had been captured.

"We need to know more about this Order," I said. "How many members could come to Wonder Falls? Is our town secretly being invaded by a secret society run by frat boys?"

Bea sat up. "What can we do? Look them up on their website? Run 'The Order' through a search engine? Ask Blake Samberg and trust he isn't lying?"

At that moment, someone knocked on the door of the hospital room.

I opened the door to find Blake waiting outside, holding a pet carrier hidden badly by his coat. Inside the carrier, Treacle put his paws against the grid of bars and meowed.

"I've made a mistake," were the first words out of Blake's mouth.

"No, I have," I said, taking Treacle from him. "Come in. Shut the door behind you."

I set the cat carrier down at the foot of the hospital bed.

Blake came into the room. I gently shut the door, turned, and slapped Blake across the face.

I was seething. "Confidant *and* informant, did you say? It was a huge mistake to trust you!"

Blake rubbed his jaw and flinched.

Bea stood up, trying to calm us both down. "I did not," she said, "just witness my cousin and soul sister assault a law enforcer!"

"As if he's to be trusted!" I was answering Bea, but my eyes were on Blake. That time, he lost our staring contest. "You're as crooked as they come, Blake Samberg."

Blake held his hands up as if he were under arrest. "Not usually. Only this time."

My jaw dropped. "Oh," I said sarcastically, "that makes it all better, then!"

"I thought I'd cracked the case. I thought that it was only about me." He glanced over at Bea. "Can I say anything more specific with her around?"

"You'd better," I said to him. "Because it's her mother who was getting assaulted while you had your showdown with Min."

Blake groaned. "I thought he wasn't going to say anything!"

Bea and I glanced at each other.

My outrage faltered as I remembered that he didn't know Treacle was my magically mind-linked pet cat—or, apparently, that I had any magic at all. I mustered up my outrage again and said, "Min Park didn't say anything about this club except that he was in it. I just figured some things out. So, tell us about the Order. No, wait, first tell us how you knew this was my cat."

Bea squatted to slide the latch open and let Treacle out of the carrier.

Blake answered, "Cats are the one thing Jake and I can talk about without fighting. He mentioned that if I saw a black cat with a star-shaped scar on its forehead, then he was probably yours."

"Right." I sat down on the edge of the hospital bed and gestured to an armchair in the corner. "Now, tell us about the Order."

Blake took his long coat off the carrier. From one pocket, he drew a palm-sized, leather-bound journal with a pyramid embossed on the cover.

"This is what they give to the legacy members of the Order. My father was a member, and he wanted me to join because he'd made some good friends there. He paid my dues at first. We host charity fundraisers, help entrepreneurs, give each other a leg up on the job network—that sort of thing. Country clubs. A few parties."

I said, "You did strike me as a party person."

"Never." He traced the triangle on the cover with his fingertips. "The pattern on this pyramid shows where in the hierarchy my father was. Until you get pretty high up, you usually only know who's immediately above you."

Bea asked, "How does the Order decide on hierarchy?"

"The higher-ups pick and choose who's going to be directly beneath them. If you progress in something called the Mysteries, then you get…"

"Higher up?" I offered.

Blake corrected me. "Deeper in. Attending solemn rituals in robes, drawing circles on the ground in chalk, dribbly candles, and saying the same thing as everybody else in the room at the same time in a language that nobody really speaks anymore."

Bea smiled. "The Mysteries! You figured out how to do magic!"

Blake's eyes flashed with resentment. "Mrs. Williams, there is no such thing. My father got too deep into it. I'm a man of science and reasoning."

I believed his last sentence. "So you don't mind if we keep that book?"

"Borrow it. I'd rather not forget how much it messed my dad up." He tossed the journal to me, and I caught it. Bea, with her magic burnout, edged her chair away. The Order journal wasn't like the Greenstone spell book, where every page and especially the cover had some seal that had to be unlocked for the magic to flow. Somebody had been careless in making it. The pulp of the pages twisted the physical world into the other worlds.

Blake continued, "I wanted out. After my father passed away, I quit paying my dues. The members would come to where I used to live and say something about legacy—how it means that you can never leave the Order. I filed complaints against them, even restraining orders, and finally I changed my name and moved here," he concluded, "where I thought that I could leave all that behind me."

"So," I said, "when you recognized the necklace—"

"I thought it was a warning from them. Min made clear that it wasn't just me who was from the Order. I met up with him in secret—I admit to that. I told Min to tell the rest of them that I was ready to barge into their chapter with guns blazing." Blake laughed. "Min's left the Order, too! They let him, though, because he wasn't a legacy. He didn't need any of their help to become a success, obviously."

I stifled a sigh of relief but still had to play it cool. "You said that you cracked the case."

From his other jacket pocket, Blake drew the chain and pyramid pendant. "Min gave me the Order's membership amulet you found. It isn't his. The pattern shows somebody too high ranking."

Bea suggested, "Could there be DNA on it still?"

"It's been passed around too much," Blake pointed out. "And Cath did say that she picked it up after the fire."

"Is it all my fault you can't catch them, then?" I demanded. "For tampering with evidence? What about the way you withheld crucial information pertaining to the case—and not for anybody else's sake but yours?"

"I'm saying that was a mistake! You don't have to forgive me, but just to start making it up to you, I thought you should be the first one to know what the next course of action is, and it won't be a DNA test." Blake stood up. "They—the Order—do have a website directory, and the Wonder Falls police force does have an IT team. We can cross-reference what I know about these patterns, what they signify, and narrow down who it might be. They might not categorize every member, but…"

I finished, "It's worth a try."

"The only problem is…" He heaved a sigh. "I'll have to tell Jake. And Chief Talbot, of course."

Bea and I started talking at the same time.

"Just do it."

"He doesn't bite!"

"Good luck."

Blake shrugged on his coat. "I just thought you deserved to know what this was all about."

I saw him out the door. "Thank you," I told him, "for trusting me with this after I slapped you. I really hope it turns out all right for you."

"I hope your Aunt Astrid gets well soon." Then Blake left.

Inside, Treacle batted at the journal with his paw.

"The Order stirs up trouble in more than the magical way," Bea remarked. "That could be all they need to get caught."

"But they have magic," I said. "They have our magic, and it's powerful!" I picked up the journal. "This has a blocking or privacy spell on it. That's why I couldn't get to Treacle when the carrier was covered. It's definitely effective, but whoever wrote the spell didn't put any safety catches on it so that it would only apply to somebody trying to read the journal. They don't know what they're doing."

"We can't get the Greenstone spell book back until we know which member of the Order came into Wonder Falls, killed Ted, and attacked my mom." Bea sighed. "You know this is the hardest thing for me to say, but we have to let them do their jobs—Blake and Jake and Talbot. Everyone."

"They can't do it properly if we don't tell them everything. They could be running out of time and not even know it!"

"Mom would know what to do." Bea brushed away a few stray wisps of hair from her mother's forehead. "I wish she'd wake up."

With that, Bea and I lapsed back into the gloomy silence we'd shared before Blake came in.

18. Trial by Fire

J ake urged Bea away from the hospital bedside, using the fact that he had a gun license and was in a better position to protect Aunt Astrid in case any agents of the Order tried to attack again.

"You think they'd attack again?" I asked him. They had what they wanted, the spell book.

Jake answered, "She might have seen something. The attacker wouldn't want to be identified."

I hadn't thought of that.

"Fine," Bea said, to my surprise.

Jake nodded. "Blake will drive you. He should be right outside."

I gave Bea a confused look.

She mouthed, "They have the book. They won't bother Aunt Astrid."

As we walked out, I whispered, "How can you be so sure?"

Seeing Blake, Bea adopted a more normal tone of voice. "They're in over their heads, drunk with power. Isn't that right, Blake? About the Order? They wouldn't hound Aunt Astrid like they did you since they don't know her personally."

"Better safe than sorry," Blake murmured.

So Blake drove Bea, Treacle, and me home. Marshmallow and Peanut Butter were already in the car. He said it would be safer if Bea and I were in the same place, and he'd stake out the house in case any members of the Order tried to attack us, just in case they were targeting everyone connected to the Brew-Ha-Ha.

The entire case had turned him and Jake into real partners again. Jake and Blake. The safety of innocent civilians was more important than arguing over attitudes.

"What makes our caution so important is that even I don't understand the motive," Blake said. "A couple of officers followed the gang violence that made up Ted Lanier's history and came to a dead end. Darren Castellan, Darla's ex-husband, has a solid alibi, and Jake says that the marriage had run its course for him—he wasn't jealous. So Ted's death had to have something to do with the Order. Why set one person on fire and leave another concussed?"

I played along. "You did say that Ted had a concussion. Maybe when Bea brought Peanut Butter home, she'd interrupted the arsonist."

"And nothing was burgled?"

I lied. "No, nothing."

Bea supplied, "It makes no sense."

"Well, Bea, Blake did describe them as basically a mob. Maybe they like to cause destruction, and they believe it's not that bad because they're all doing it together and laughing about it afterward." I reasoned, "They'll still go about it in different ways because they're different people."

The car pulled into my driveway. Bea carried Marshmallow in the cage into my house, with Treacle and Peanut Butter following.

Blake stopped me at the door. "I can't shake the feeling that you're holding out on me, Cath. After today, I swear I have no secrets from you."

"I don't have secrets, either. I never did! I have privates." That sounded really bad, didn't it? I blamed Blake's cheekbones and the composition of the rest of his face for distracting me. A hint of a smile appeared on his face; he wanted to laugh. Wearily, I added, "You know what I mean. Secrets. The day's not over until I've had some sleep. Then we'll talk. Yeah?" Without waiting for a reply, I patted his arm and walked past him.

Treacle walked me up to my room. *"In the cellar below the place where the fire happened, I smelled something."*

I wanted to theorize and think some more until everything fell into place, but I was too exhausted. I fell into bed without changing my clothes.

I dreamed that Aunt Astrid and the Maid of the Mist were one person, and I felt silly for not realizing that they were. Her braids cascaded in a loud hiss of flowing water that sounded like rain. From the balcony of the Parks' grocery store, I watched a meteor shaped like the pyramid pendant of the Order tumble from the sky and crash into the estuary of the three waterfalls.

Blake stood at a chalkboard like a teacher and said, "But you see, it isn't possible for this to happen."

From my school desk, I raised my hand so I could take my turn to talk. "It did happen. My Aunt Astrid is in the hospital now because of it. You said the Order did this."

Blake shook his head and looked around. "Does anybody else know the correct answer? The Maid of the Mist."

Aunt Astrid, in the seat beside me, wasn't raising her hand. She looked right at me and said, "I'm waking up."

"What?" I asked, confused and hopeful.

As if repeating herself even though she was not, Aunt Astrid said, "Sometimes, the future that I see is fixed."

"I refuse to believe that," declared a voice from my other side. I turned to see Darla Castellan as she'd appeared in high school. More quietly, she suggested, "Senior moment yesterday, maybe?" Darla swung her arm as if to strike me, holding a shoe with a strangely shaped heel—a kitten heel, they call it. I ducked, and the shoe flew past me.

"Aunt Astrid!" I shouted. I should have taken that hit. If only I hadn't been somewhere else...

But where Aunt Astrid had been sitting, Ted Lanier sat, pressing star-shaped cookie cutters into a piece of rolled-out dough.

Bea took the seat on his other side. She gloomily added, "We're at stake. As witches have a historical tendency to be. Ha. Ha. Ha."

At her final "ha," Ted burst into flames. In an instant, the friendly face I'd known in life became the charred remains I'd caught sight of.

At that, I stood up. "I'm done with this." I turned to leave and entered a ballroom instead of a classroom. Everything was made of glossy marble. Walking was difficult in the ball gown I was wearing.

Min Park stood in the middle of the room, looking perfect in a white tuxedo. "Do you dance?" he asked, extending his hand toward me.

Music filled the room—but it wasn't music. It sounded like several people intoning the same thing at the same time in a language so old that nobody should speak it anymore.

"I don't know what this dance is called," I told Min.

He put one hand on my waist and held one of my hands with the other. "Trial by water," Min answered. "One, two, three. One, two, three. Repeating history."

"No." I laughed as we danced. "I'm pretty sure that this is called a…" *Waltz* was the word, but I forgot it in the dream. "A waterfall?" I looked down at our feet to make sure I wasn't stepping on his and he wasn't stepping on mine.

Our foot maneuvers looked strange. He seemed to be stepping where I had just stepped. It didn't make sense. His shoes were nice, though.

I looked up to see that my dance partner was Blake, not Min.

"We were all under orders," he said to me. "Dress code. Bloodline legacy. What to say, how to think—it's a cult that takes over your life."

I didn't know what to say to that, so I asked him, "What's this dance called again?"

Blake stepped back and moved my hand in a circle, signaling me to spin around. I did so, and Reuben Connors in his fireman gear pulled me to his chest and answered, "Trial by fire."

I shouted in surprise and struggled to push him away.

I woke up struggling against the quilt.

19. The Social Network

As Bea filled the food and water dishes for all three cats, I made pancakes and eyed the morning sky suspiciously from the kitchen window. The sun shone bright over the neighbors walking their dogs, the shingles of the suburban houses, and the police cars as they drove by on their ways to Aunt Astrid's home.

As Bea filled the food and water dishes for all three cats, I made pancakes and eyed the morning sky suspiciously from the kitchen window. The sun shone bright over the neighbors walking their dogs, the shingles of the suburban houses, and the police cars driving by on their way to Aunt Astrid's home.

When the pancakes stacked higher than the distance between Bea's elbow and her wrist, she yelled at me to stop.

"What are they waiting for?" I wondered aloud. "They have what they wanted, our spell book. Why aren't they using it?" I ate my pancakes over the countertop by the sink so I could keep looking at the sky suspiciously.

Bea, at the table, spooned maple sugar over her pancakes and bacon. "I don't know," she admitted. "I've read that book from cover to cover—only once, but..." Bea didn't need to be so modest. She had a great memory for everything she read. "I can only guess that every one of those spells comes at too high a cost for them. It isn't just a spell book. It's almost a how-to manual on different human sacrifices!"

"Between Ted and Aunt Astrid, the Order obviously isn't squeamish about hurting other people." I remembered what Treacle had told me the night before. "Treacle did some investigating, too. He smelled something in Aunt Astrid's nuclear bunker. Forensics probably wouldn't think to look for it, and I wouldn't even recognize it with my human nose."

Treacle and Peanut Butter sniffed each other's noses. Then Treacle, on a mission and tail up, stalked out the door.

The doorbell rang. I started, grabbed for something in the kitchen that I could use as a weapon, and bolted after Treacle.

"Cath, calm down!" Bea called after me.

Through the door, I could hear Jake's laughter and a voice that sounded like Blake's except that it was happy. I recognized it as Blake's for certain when he said, "Okay. Bye, kitty!"

I opened the door as Bea jogged up to me.

"Cath," she said, wrenching my weapon from my hand, "that's an egg beater!"

I had dripped pancake batter all down the hall. Peanut Butter was licking it off the floor behind me.

Jake looked from Bea to me and back. "Either way, Cath wasn't going to hurt us."

"Rough night?" Blake ventured.

"Good morning," I answered stubbornly. "I made too many pancakes. Please come in and eat some."

Blake and I went down the hall first.

Bea took her husband's hand and murmured, "They're both learning human ways!"

"I know! I'm so proud," Jake murmured back.

I turned to glower at them. "I can hear you!" Just because I wasn't a social butterfly like Bea, that didn't mean I was socially awkward.

We all sat at the kitchen table. Bea bustled about, being the good hostess, getting the extra glasses and asking who was on shift or stakeout to guard her mother.

I should have been the one making our guests comfortable and asking those questions, but I was too busy wracking my brain for why the Order would wait to cast such powerful spells as the ones in our spell book.

Jake spoke first. "The lead with the Order was a major breakthrough."

"Don't get their hopes up," Blake said to him. "The social network on the Order's official website doesn't list everyone. Min Park wasn't on it because he quit lickety-split, and some higher-up members get certain privileges."

"It's still further than we would have gotten in two days following French organized crime syndicates." Jake gave Blake the look I imagine fathers give their sons to remind them of something they'd been scolded for, and I realized Blake was still covering for me. Jake might have known I was investigating privately, but if he'd known I'd tampered with evidence... Well, Jake just might have found it in himself to be meaner.

"The Order is exclusive," Blake said. "They're superstitious but not any less macho."

"So?" I said. "Would they break into Aunt Astrid's home, attack her, even kill her chef, just because she did tarot card readings and tea leaf readings? Why not start killing in Sedona? Or Glastonbury, on the other side of the pond?"

"That's what we're trying to say," Jake said. "Mrs. Colette Lanier had a reputation in her town for giving astrology readings, up until her death from cyanide-poisoned biscuits."

"That were star-shaped," Blake scoffed. "It's just the sort of message the Order would send. Those cowards!"

Jake nodded. "The Order has a worldwide network. Maybe it wasn't Ted's dad who crossed the wrong people, but his mom."

Bea and I looked at each other. I knew we were both thinking the same thing. She and I have had to hide that we were witches all our lives. Aunt Astrid let it slip a little for harmless fun, and someone broke into her home and attacked her. Mrs. Lanier was poisoned to death, and we don't even know if she was a real witch. But the Order was allowed to have an online social network. It wasn't fair.

"New legacy," Blake said ponderously. "New blood, new people, new initiative, new mode of operations… and judging from their lodges—which have gone into disrepair since my old man's time—not as many resources to cover up their criminal ventures. You can only pull strings to get someone out of jail from outside of jail."

"We've got security on high alert both around the perimeter of this house and around your mother's hospital room," Jake assured his wife.

Bea said, "I still want to stay with her. Maybe my being there would help."

I knew it would help Astrid. I was just afraid of what it would do to Bea. "Take Marshmallow with you," I said to her.

Jake looked doubtful. "I don't think having a cat in the hospital room would be very hygienic—"

"But Mom loves Marshmallow," Bea said.

I said, "She needs the drip removed and a vet's checkup, too. Aunt Astrid wanted to have him groomed the day of the fire, but she was too tired."

"If he's groomed first, it should be fine," Blake added. "Besides, what's a hospital but a vet for people? And you never hear at a vet's that it's not hygienic to have people running around."

I wouldn't have put it that way, and maybe Jake was already convinced, but in any case, after that, Jake and Bea left with Marshmallow.

Blake saw them off then turned to ask me what I'd been hiding from him. I knew he would. He'd prepared me without knowing it.

I interrupted, "Have you logged into your account on the Order's website?"

He looked at me with surprise.

"Really? Had nobody in the police department thought of that?"

20. Rejoining the Brotherhood

The Wonder Falls Police Department outsourced its computer savvy to Winnifred Hansen, whose image matched the wholesomeness of her name. She made video tutorials for quilting and knitting that Aunt Astrid loved. I hadn't known she'd also coded and designed the websites for every major business in Wonder Falls. She knew a lot more about computers than that too, if you can believe it.

Blake and I met the middle-aged Mrs. Hansen at her house to tell her our plan. For someone on the cutting edge of technology, she wasn't much for getting straight to business. She made Blake and me coffee and suggested that the Brew-Ha-Ha be made into an Internet café.

"Forget the small-town charm of Old Wonder Falls," she told me. "I haven't seen the sun in days, and I'm just fine."

Blake faked a cough to tell me to be cautious.

Winnifred caught it instantly. "Hey," she said, "I'm helping your investigation, aren't I?" She grinned mischievously. "So, if some whippersnapper with an entrepreneurial spirit and a lousy attitude finds her website under"—the next part was lost in a whirlwind of jargon that I doubt even Bea would have been able to decipher—"and it's allegedly by me, then what are you going to do?"

"We've got laws against that," Blake objected. "I would not recommend it."

I understood the first part, or I thought I did—Darla. I'm not the only one in town who doesn't take to Darla Castellan.

"I understand that the lady in question has that effect on people," I told Mrs. Hansen sympathetically. Of course, I'd never done magic to ruin Darla's life, and hacking might as well be something like magic done by nonwitches. I felt a little guilty, egging on Mrs. Hansen to use her skills against someone else, so I added, "She'd be more occupied by her divorce proceedings, I've heard."

"Oh," Mrs. Hansen said. "I've been divorced a few times. It's a hassle, I can tell you. I'll go easy on her from now on, then. Goodness knows there's been worse than her in town, lately."

That prompted us to remind her of the Order, and she led us into her den, where her computer was. After that, Blake simply had to sit down and type.

After he'd logged in, Mrs. Hansen nudged him aside and set about browsing. She observed, "Well, Detective Samberg, if you were afraid of stalkers, I can tell you not to worry. The permissions on your account say 'sour grapes' to me!"

I asked, "What does that mean? Is Blake's account no good?"

"Not entirely. I have more access now than I've had for hours, but everything important is encrypted. Of course it is. Whether I try to figure out which members of this site might be in Wonder Falls or who else in Wonder Falls might be on this site…" Mrs. Hansen shrugged. "I only have two hands."

Blake sighed, but not with relief. He said, "I know what would make this easier. Excuse me, Mrs. Hansen…"

Blake went to a chat box and typed, "Moved to Wonder Falls. Done some thinking. Time to rejoin the brotherhood."

"Are you sure about this?" I asked Blake.

Blake shook his head.

I took his hand. "Then don't do it."

"But there are innocent people being attacked," Blake murmured.

I drew myself up. "You shouldn't be one of them. I don't want you to be one of them!"

Mrs. Hansen scoffed, reached over, and pressed the Enter key.

"Mrs. Hansen!" I shrieked.

"Oh, spare me. Samberg knew what would make this easier. He was right."

Blake stared at the screen in mute horror, so I spoke up. "You're out of line! Those are very dangerous people!"

"You think that was out of line? Honey, you haven't seen anything yet." Winnifred typed a string of numbers I didn't recognize, followed by the words, "Message me."

Blake found his voice too late. After Mrs. Hansen put that message through, he said, "That's my cell-phone number."

"Consider it a burner." Mrs. Hansen looked him over and said sarcastically, "Oh, I'm sorry, I didn't realize you had such a full address book and active social life."

Blake's phone rang. He leaped up and backed away as if a dog were attacking him. He wriggled his phone out of his pocket and threw it in the air.

I caught it. "Calm down, Blake! I'll answer it. They'll think it's a wrong number and hang up."

"No!" Blake said. "They'll hunt you down for that alone. Give it back to me. I'll play along with them until we can get them behind bars."

I lobbed the phone back at him. He caught it, steeled himself, and then crumpled. "I can't. I can't do it."

I wrenched the phone from him and actually looked at the screen that time. "Oh, it's just Jake." I answered the phone. "Hi, Ja—"

"There's been another fire," Jake said. "Meet me at 78 Whitewater Street, corner of Black Lake Bank. It's in Old Wonder Falls."

"That's Nadia LaChance's place!" I said.

"Cath?"

I tossed the phone to Blake, who caught it and said, "Yeah, I'm on the move. Mrs. Hansen?"

Mrs. Hansen had begun typing furiously. "See yourselves out. Lock the door behind you. I'll call Chief Talbot if anything comes up, and you're welcome for the coffee."

On the way out, Blake asked me, "Who's Nadia LaChance?"

"At the insurance office yesterday morning— you couldn't have missed her," I said to him. "She's the closest Wonder Falls town ever came to having a Goth girl, so she stuck with that fashion all the way through her twenties. The Order's really scraping the barrel, aren't they? If they're targeting anybody who looks the slightest bit like they believe in magic, should we be guarding the kindergarten next?"

"It must be more than that," Blake said. "Cath, what aren't you saying?"

"She hates my guts. She has ever since…"— well, scratch that theory—"yesterday, after the fire. Umm…" What else was there to say? "She has a live-in girlfriend, so this could be a hate crime. She has an artistic Bohemian twin sister."

Blake took all that in. "Maybe she and her twin dress up like each other to trick people, and one of them is evil."

"Now *that's* scraping the barrel!"

21. Another Attack

When Blake and I arrived, I was horrified at catching sight of Treacle on the second-story balcony of Nadia's house.

"I found the smell! What I smelled yesterday!" Treacle thought to me. *"She's still inside!"* Treacle sent me an image of the interior of the house.

"Treacle, get out of there!" I thought.

"She fed me treats! She always does! When she didn't this time, I knew it was because of these other people who came downstairs and went away. They left the door open, so I went upstairs and found her like this. They started this fire. Maybe she saw their faces!"

Out in front, the fire brigade seemed to be having some problems with the nearest hydrant. Reuben Connors was almost laughing. "Let it burn out! It'll be fine."

Blake was just looking in the direction I was—he didn't know what Treacle had told me. "He's a smart cat," Blake said. "He'll find his own way out. Cath?"

I glowered at Reuben, looked back at the balcony, steeled myself, and—despite Blake's protests—ran into the burning building.

The smoke and ash stung my eyes, and the heat was like an oven. I pulled the front of my shirt over my nose and mouth so I could breathe and ran through the fire as quickly as I could. Flames won't burn unless you actually touch them for more than three seconds, but they were growing, and I was surprised by how quickly I ran out of air because the smoke was so thick. I felt I was drowning without any water.

When I got to the bedroom, I was squinting so hard I had to close my eyes and just feel around for the body. The image Treacle had sent me helped, but at that moment, I wondered if I'd gotten myself into real trouble.

I felt a leg then an arm. No time to check whether she'd broken any bones or bled out anywhere—I couldn't see a thing.

I hauled the slackened body up and heard something drop, like a phone—maybe she had called the fire brigade herself. Then I half dragged, half carried Nadia to the balcony. On my back, she shifted. Good. She was still alive.

I took a huge, gasping inhalation of open air. It wasn't exactly fresh because it was still tainted by enough ash and smoke to make me cough.

The long ladder from the fire truck reached the balcony. Treacle hopped onto the roof, took a running start, and leaped. He landed safely in the sprawling branches of a nearby maple tree and scurried the rest of the way down.

Nadia had regained consciousness by the time we reached the ground again. The rescue left parts of my skin feeling as though I had awful sunburn, and even though I was glad I could breathe again, few smells are fouler than singed hair.

Nadia shook off the firefighters who tried to get her onto a gurney and into the ambulance or even to give her a blanket. She walked toward me. "They say you ran in to save me while the place was on fire," she said. "I guess you're not so bad after all."

I guess you're not so bad after all? I gave her a disdainful blink. "Gosh, Nadia, can you hold a grudge or something?" I had to remember she might have stolen the book.

"Hey," Nadia chuckled, "I'm not like your cousin. I'm not made of hugs, you know?"

"Nadia!" Ruby elbowed her way past Fire Chief Gillian and tottered over to throw her arms around Nadia. "You should have gone shopping with Darla and me! This never would have happened."

"I have no regrets," Nadia said flatly. "She spent the night here to talk about nothing but herself. We're too old for slumber parties, and a few seconds was always too much Darla for me."

"Nobody actually lives in this part of Old Wonder Falls anymore," I said. "The whole block could have gone up in flames before someone other than Nadia phoned the fire brigade. Great thing you got this place insured, huh?"

Ruby grumbled, "Processing takes a while, at least in Sutherland's hands. But I'm so glad you're safe!" She hugged Nadia again. The smell of artificial jasmine cut through the smell of burnt hair. She pulled away enough to ask, "You shouldn't have called if that meant it left you smothered almost to death!"

Nadia said, "Those jerks broke my cell phone! I wasn't about to wander around alone looking for a phone booth."

I asked her, "Did you see who might have done this, then?"

"Yeah!" Nadia said. "They weren't from around here. I clawed this one guy's stocking off his head, and I didn't hit my head or anything."

"I'll go and get you a lineup, then." I edged away and wandered the crowd.

Treacle found me.

"That," I told Treacle, *"was very reckless of you."*

"We're closer to the truth!" Treacle objected.

"We're too far from anything that makes sense!" I thought back to the beginning—Ted Lanier had been given a concussion and the Brew-Ha-Ha set on fire in predawn morning. Aunt Astrid was given a concussion in her own home—but no fire—and the attack had happened in the early evening. Nadia LaChance, in her own home, had no concussion, and the attack had taken place at noon. If there was a group of agents from the Order doing this, then maybe they were working in shifts.

I needed Blake.

"Blake!" I called out to the crowd, but I couldn't find him. I picked Treacle up. "Blake! Samberg!"

One of the police cars had its driver's window rolled down. When the police radio on the dashboard started its static sound, I picked it up.

Jake was saying, "Samberg, please copy!"

So it was Blake's car.

"The fire's done," I told Jake. "It was definitely the Order's doing, but Nadia's alive—able and willing to identify them. Did you try Blake's phone? I can't find him either."

"His cell's busy. We're the only people he knows!"

My heart sank. "We're not the only people who know his number, though."

22. Human Sacrifice

The guys spent the rest of the afternoon getting Nadia's statement. I left Treacle with Peanut Butter at my place and went to the hospital. Aunt Astrid still hadn't woken up. I told Bea about that morning.

Bea was aghast. "But the Order has the book! The real one! Why bother attacking people who have nothing to do with it?"

I wondered for a moment. "Well, you did say that a lot of the spells needed a human sacrifice. Can you tell me more about them?"

"These spells were written in the medieval age. They took into account if the moon was void or what planet ruled the hour of the spell."

"That sounds complicated!"

"If none of the members of the Order were like us, basically born into magic and having to feel out for the right conditions and walk in the other worlds—they might want to do it by the book." Bea thought about it some more. "They could capture a human sacrifice to have ready, but Nadia wasn't captured, was she?"

"No. It's a good thing she wasn't concussed before they tried to burn her alive." I thought about it. "Actually, I think that makes the Order real sadists."

Bea nodded. "To save nonwitches from the horrible reality of magic, the old Greenstones always, always made sure that the sacrifice came from somebody within the coven."

"Do you think somebody would volunteer to be a human sacrifice?"

"If everybody else in the coven treated it like some great honor, then I wouldn't be surprised. But the way the book was written, it had to be the life of a sister."

"Or," I said, "a brother." I began to panic. "They wouldn't know how much bloodlines have to do with it, would they? They'd only see 'sisterhood' and think 'brotherhood' would be better. They lured Blake away. They captured him. They're going to kill him!"

Bea stood up. "If that spell succeeds, this might be the least of our worries. If it fails— say they don't have magic or something—then they'll try again, and we need to warn Min."

I nodded, relieved that my panic finally had a direction. "I'll call Min. You call Jake."

I tried Mrs. Park's number first. She told me that Min had gotten used to the bachelor's lifestyle, so he had rented an inn room of his own. She couldn't hide how relieved she was that I hadn't joined him.

I couldn't help but break down and cry. "My beloved aunt, who's been like a mother to me, was attacked last night! A gang of thugs won't quit terrorizing my family and our friends!"

"Cath, I'm so sorry," Mrs Park said. "I didn't know about Astrid."

"I should have warned you all," I told her. "You've been friends of my family, too. You've got to stay safe, all right? I mean it. Try to get Min to stay over with you until the culprits are behind bars."

"All right."

When I hung up the phone, Bea looked bleak.

"We're too late," she said to me. "Jake says that Blake called the police station. They recorded the call. You're not going to like what he said."

23. A Failsafe

I bribed one of the nurses to take care of Marshmallow, and Bea and I left the hospital room for the police station.

Chief Talbot greeted us as we came in through the door. "Miss Greenstone, Mrs. Williams."

"Is Detective Samberg safe, then?" I said, confused. "Bea only said on the way that he called for me. Why didn't he call me directly? What did Jake mean by us being 'too late'?"

"Come with me."

The Wonder Falls police force, along with Nadia, was clustered around a recorder to listen in on a call.

"Only four voices in the background," Nadia said. "I can remember each and every one of them."

"Right," Jake said. "Ready to play it back again?"

Nadia gave me a pitying look. Bea put her arm around my shoulder.

Jake started the recording.

"I'm calling to say that I've found the real power in this town." The voice was Blake's, but the words couldn't have been. "It's me. My birthright. The way was mapped by my father, and I walk it with my brothers!"

Three voices in the background whooped and roared in encouragement.

"We are beyond the reach of the law, and come midnight tonight, we'll be the rulers and not the subjects of nature itself."

Another voice shouted, "Help me!"

Bea and I both gasped.

"That's Min," I said.

Blake's voice continued, "Tell Cath that I knew she was holding out on me. If this pathetic little wimp—"

"Pipsqueak!" said a voice in the background.

"Reuben," Nadia said with grim certainty, identifying the voice.

"—is her idea of a worthwhile partner, then I give up. He's not the prince, doll! He's the damsel. Would you tell her that for me? Would you tell Cath?"

Jake's voice answered on the recording: "You can tell her yourself. I'll bring her in. Just give me an hour."

"An hour? Yeah. We'll be waiting."

"Man, no." That was Reuben's voice. "They'll figure out where we are by then."

"That's hard to do when we're moving! Back down, underling." Blake replied to Jake, "Half an hour. It can't be hard to hurry. This is a small town. There. That's the end of it. Move."

"Not again!" Min's voice sounded muffled.

Reuben's voice objected, "I'm serious, bro. You might be some hotshot legacy member of the Order, but we're not going to wait on your ex-girlfriend! We've gone too far waiting for this. If you think you can just come in here—" A scuffling noise was heard, then the line went dead.

I breathed a sigh of relief. "All right. Blake's bought us time."

"Wait, what?" Nadia said to me. She sat upright, a confused expression on her face. "Do you even speak English? Your beau's a traitor and a nutcase!"

"He called the police station when he could have called me," I said. "Blake knew to get the message out to the greatest number of people with the best skills to cover the most ground. They're on the move, right? But did you hear any vehicles, any footsteps?"

Jake answered, "No."

I nodded. "When Blake told the others to get a move on, Min said, 'Not again!' because Reuben had done this to him before! He put Min in a burlap sack and sent him downriver."

"And," Bea added, lying, "from what Blake told us of the Order's rites of black magic…"

I completed the sentence, "Min Park is to be their human sacrifice. There's a ritual they're going to try to do, to gain control over the forces of nature. 'Come midnight tonight, we'll be the rulers and not the subjects of nature itself.' What's the grandest display of natural beauty and power that's closest to this town? The falls!"

"We have until midnight," Bea said. "The traditional sort of rituals that Blake told us about are very particular about it being done at a particular time."

"All right!" Chief Talbot said. "Let's get a move on!"

Bea caught up with Jake first. "Remember what I told you about not getting shot or killed."

He kissed her, broke away, and strapped on his holster and gun.

I sidled up to Bea. "The spell could work," I said. "Our police force won't be prepared for it. They think the Order are deluded and the magic isn't real. Even Blake still thinks so."

Bea nodded. "We have to get there first and stop the ritual. Keep the secret."

"This is about more than keeping the secret," I told her. "This is about not waking the Maid of the Mist. The other world of magic can't cross over into this place." I added regretfully, "And you can't come with me."

"What? No." Bea turned to face me. "Cath, your mother tried to stop something from crossing over. She tried to do that all on her own, and that killed her. That was just using the common magic that every witch knows to guard the boundaries between the nonwitch world and the other. This is trying to stop a big spell."

"I'm not going to stop something from crossing over," I said, "I'm going to stop a bunch of jerks from calling it over. The police will do the rest. Everybody knows that I'm a loose cannon and impulsive."

"I'll just say that you dragged me into it, that I went along to try to curb your heroism!"

"Then we won't have a failsafe! You've got to take Aunt Astrid and the cats and head for high ground in some sturdy building. If I fail to stop the Order, something horrible is going to happen."

"But you..." Bea's sad, panicked eyes looked from me to her husband. "And Jake..."

"I'll do my best," I said to her. "But if my best isn't good enough, then you're our last hope to get that book back. That means you have to live. I'm sorry that we can't warn Jake."

I walked over to Chief Talbot. "Is there anything else I can do to help?"

He answered, "You've done plenty. We could use more people on the ground, though, so maybe you can take a message to the investigators at your Aunt Astrid's place?" He hollered to another officer, "Boone! Call everyone back from Min's room at the inn."

I followed Boone and his partner out of the police station, planning to visit Min's room at the inn on my own.

24. A Visit to the Inn

I thought that if Min had kept the necklace just because he thought it looked neat, then he'd have kept something I would be able to use, too.

When I was sure the police had been called away for a search of the area around the falls, I sneaked into the inn room.

I stole a black hooded robe from Min's luggage, which I pulled on over my clothes, and in the inside pocket of the robe, I hid Blake's father's journal.

On the way out, the sky rumbled, making me look up to see the storm clouds heading our way.

I avoided the police by sending out a mental call for every cat to either stay and help or head for the hills. The ones that chose to stay volunteered to be distractions or warnings.

That's how I made my way through the town and then through the woods and then to a simple boat tied to a pier by the lake. I boarded the boat and untied it.

When the clouds rolled past the moon, I got out the journal and flipped through the pages even though a spell had caught my eye already. "If found, please return," I recited. "This prized possession's tether burn."

In my mind's eye, invisible to any nonwitches, a perfect line of bright magic shot from the journal over to where Blake would be. I tucked the journal into the robe's inside pocket again, took up the oar I'd found in the boat, and paddled as fast as I could in the direction of the magic.

Midnight—the witching hour—approached.

25. The Witching Hour

B ea returned to the hospital with Peanut Butter and Treacle at her heels.

The nurse I'd bribed on the way out tried to stop her. "Really, three cats! Mrs. Williams, that's too much! You can tell Miss Greenstone to keep her money and whatever favors she made up—"

"Actually, I can't," Bea said. "Don't worry. We're leaving."

Everybody in town knew Bea as the nice one, the sweet one. Her terseness surprised the young nurse into silence.

In Astrid's hospital room, Marshmallow sat upright and stretched when Bea entered.

"Ready?" Bea asked the cats. Awkwardly, she added. "I won't know if you are, because I'm not Cath. I don't speak Cat. I don't even know if you speak Human. But I need you to make magic—all three of you, not just Marshmallow. Can you do that?"

Peanut Butter meowed and jumped onto Aunt Astrid's hospital bed, followed by Treacle.

"I'll take that as a yes." Bea intoned, "Blood calls to blood, spirit to soul. This healer commands it: make my mother whole!"

A blast of magic rippled from the hospital bed.

Bea almost fainted with the effort. She steadied herself on the bar beside the hospital bed and looked toward her mother.

Astrid groaned. Beneath her eyelids, something moved.

"Mom!" Bea exclaimed.

Astrid was barely strong enough and alert enough to form words. "Don't… take the book…"

Bea flinched. "Yeah… about that…"

Astrid opened her eyes and looked at Bea worriedly. "Where's Cath?"

"She's out there doing her best with some crazy Cath plan that only Cath could think up, let alone go through with," Bea told her mother. "You and I need to get out of her way and out of the way of everybody who might be in Cath's way."

"What's she planning? What's she done?" Astrid groaned, struggling to sit upright in the bed.

Later, I realized Aunt Astrid wasn't talking about me at that point.

"That will be a great thing to discuss," Bea told her, "at the Parks' place uphill."

"First, I need to tell the police who attacked me."

"We already know. The Order, wasn't it?"

"What order?"

"Strange men led by Reuben Connors? Or did he shake off his henchmen and rob our home all on his own?"

Astrid shook her head.

The thread of magic led me to a yacht floating between two of the three falls. A searchlight mounted on its mast swept back and forth across the turbulent waters. I let my borrowed boat float into it and heard two unfamiliar voices call out above the roar of the nearby falls.

"Let me talk to him!" Blake shouted. "This is Legacy business."

I pulled the hood of the cloak further over my face, and I held the journal up and out into the searchlight.

"See?" Blake said. "Dexter, stand over at the starboard side. Felix, stand over at the port side. Look smart, both of you. We're welcoming a grand master."

I tried to stand and move in as grand and masterly a way as possible as I tied the stolen boat to the yacht and stepped off it, up the ladder, and onto the deck.

Blake was there to greet me in a black hooded robe of his own.

"Cath, what are you doing?" Blake hissed.

"I had to make sure that Min was all right. Please say you still have your gun!"

"That thug, Reuben Connors… he took it. He's below deck with Min right now, so you can be sure that Mr. Park is not all right. What's taking backup so long?"

"Maybe if you signaled with your handy searchlight!"

"I can't signal without these two mooks knowing that I'm signaling."

"Well, there's two of us, and there's two of them now, isn't there?"

One of the mooks piped up, "I don't like all these strange people showing up and claiming to be from the Order."

Blake rolled his eyes. "Silence, underling!"

"No, Felix has got a point," said the other mook, who must have been Dexter. "If anybody should be talking to the grand master, it's Reuben."

I told Blake, "We'll catch them off their guard. I'll take Dexter."

Blake turned to the two mooks. "The grand master would meet with this accomplished brother! Fetch him!"

As Felix made his way below deck, I pocketed the journal, strode toward Dexter, pulled his hood down, and shoved him overboard. The element of surprise—and the adrenaline rush—made up for how much bigger he was than me. He yelled much more loudly than I'd expected as he tumbled and splashed into the water.

I lowered my hood, shrugged off the robe, and handed Blake the journal. "That's bound to draw attention."

"I'll keep the other two distracted," Blake said. "Can you climb the mast?"

"Like a cat!"

"Good. Signal with the searchlight. Go!"

As I climbed, Felix and Reuben came up from belowdecks.

"What did you do, Samberg?"

Blake met his gaze and set his jaw. "Dexter and I got into a scuffle. I wanted to see how dexterous he really was. As it turns out, not awfully."

"Felix says that a grand master of the Order came on board."

Blake laughed. "Why'd you go and tell the boss a foolish thing like that? You know he wanted to have some uninterrupted time with Park."

From the searchlight, I saw a glint of metal as Reuben drew his gun.

A shot sounded.

"No!" I screamed.

Another shot sounded, and the searchlight shattered into darkness.

Reuben's voice taunted, "Here, kitty, kitty, kitty. I've got your boyfriend. Both of them! I've got your book! So you'd better come on out."

A cloud shifted so the light of the full moon washed the deck.

I climbed down and stood behind the unlucky Felix, who'd been shot in the head. "Why did you do this?" I asked Reuben, trying to keep the tremor out of my voice. Min was crumpled on the ground.

"I wanted uninterrupted fun time with Min Park and Cath Greenstone and..." Reuben turned to look at Blake. "Actually, you can go." He sighted down the barrel at Blake.

"Don't you dare!" I shouted.

Reuben laughed. "Oh, come on! I don't want you ganging up on me. I'm just one person, and there's three of you. Bullies!"

I looked at Min, whom Reuben was grasping by the collar of his shirt. Min had ropes around his wrists and ankles and a gag over his mouth.

I said, "You were always the bully, Reuben Connors."

"Oh, yeah?" Reuben yanked Min's gag down. "Hey, Min, buddy. Why don't you tell Cath Greenstone what you said about me?"

"I say a lot of things about you," Min admitted.

"When we met up as brothers of the Order. Can you remember?"

Min shook his head.

Reuben said, "Min said that the Order obviously wasn't as elite and exclusive as they advertised, just because I was in it. How about that? My family called me a bad seed. I traveled around, tried to find the good in me, made friends in the Order... and this chink, who's got everything handed to him on a silver platter, says that I'm just dirt."

"You made life in this town awful for Min!" I shouted. "You make it awful for your sister. You've made it awful for me and my family for the past three days!"

"Welcome to the real world!" Reuben retorted. "The people who win are the ones who take power and keep it from everybody else. Don't act nice and pretend that you don't know it. Isn't that what the book is about?" With a nudge of his gun in my direction, I looked down and realized that Felix had been holding the Greenstone spell book.

"Pick it up," Reuben ordered. "The grand master of the Order gave me a talk, you know. Exactly what Min said—they wanted better than me. I said that I was the only one who could get them exactly what the Order really needed."

Blake spoke up. "What was that?"

"Real magic." Sharply, Reuben said to me, "Didn't I tell you to pick up that book?"

"If you shoot me," I said, "you'll be short one person to say the incantation, and I'm the only one here who's a natural-born witch."

"Cath?" Blake looked confusedly at me.

"Right." Reuben turned the gun on Blake. "Like all the Greenstones. Three people in a coven. Three cats. Three waterfalls. Three people to say the spell. If one backs out, every single one of us on this boat dies. I have the gun, remember?"

I glowered at him.

"Of course!" Reuben laughed, remembering. "Min's going to die either way. You don't care so much for your life, and you're the type who would take me down with you and tell yourself it's worth it. But if you do as I say, then Blake just might live."

"If I do as you say," I argued, "no one lives. You're in over your head! The forces of nature never answer to someone who doesn't respect them!"

Reuben scoffed and nudged Min. "Women! That's what killed Ted in the end, you know. A treacherous woman."

Blake cleared his throat. "I think it was a big, burly thug who broke his head open and burned him up."

"Yeah, it was," I said to Reuben. "What on earth are you talking about? If you hate women so much, then I should be the sacrifice," I told Reuben. "I'll be the one sure to die instead of Min."

Reuben considered it for a moment. Then his phone alarm went off. He shut it off. "Ten minutes to midnight. How long does it take for a sacrifice to die from drowning?" He hauled Min up by the collar, dragging Min's back against the yacht's railing. "Because I don't do eleventh-hour changes in plans."

"Don't do this, Reuben!" I shouted as Min struggled against him.

Sarcastically, Reuben said, "Oh, okay. If you say so." He scoffed and shoved Min overboard. Over the roar of the falls, I heard the splash.

I saw a loop of rope hanging on the railing of the yacht, where nothing had been before, and knew that Min had managed to tie it while Reuben and I were talking. Still, there'd been a splash. Min was underwater, tied up so he couldn't swim, and I couldn't pull him up. I reached my mind out to any animals in the area, but the roar of the churning waters and my own screams drowned out my attempts.

Reuben aimed the gun at Blake. "Stand beside Cath. Turn to the Wakening Waterfalls ritual and start reading! Now!"

I pulled the spell book from Felix's hands and flipped through the pages quickly. Blake sidled up beside me, and I traced my index finger below the words so he could follow. Blake caught on with the repetition—and, unfortunately, so did Reuben.

Our voices joined in a chorus, and I hoped Min was managing to stay afloat somehow. Without his life, the three of us could say the words until dawn but the spell wouldn't work.

However, the water began to glow.

I let my voice keep on chanting on autopilot to catch sight of Blake's expression. He looked at the water, too, disbelieving.

The other world had crossed over.

Tragically, that could be possible only if Min had drowned to death.

Tears fell from my eyes as a pillar of light exploded from the center of the lake into the sky. The book dropped from my hands. The spell was complete.

"Cath, are you seeing this?" Blake wondered.

"Bravo, Cath!" Reuben said to me. "It's too bad we'll have to share this power among the three of us, work in harmony or something. Can you imagine working in harmony with him?" Reuben gestured at Blake. "Actually," Reuben said, "now that it's done, why don't I kill the both of you and just do whatever I want with this portal of power? That's not my holy book, after all."

"It would kill you," I told him.

"Oh, Cath. I've found out so many of your precious secrets. Do you want to know one of mine?"

"Taking in that much power would kill you," I told him again with certainty. "And the Maid of the Mist will flood the town and kill everyone in it. She only speaks to the Greenstones in her dreams, in our dreams. Even that's too much for us. You do not want to wake her up!"

To that, Reuben replied, "I don't care. For once, I did something great." He aimed his gun at me.

Blake pushed me aside, and the shot missed.

"Go!" Blake shouted, "Get back to the boat and get out of here!"

Didn't he know a magic spell in action when he saw it? The town was doomed. This yacht was doomed. That tiny wooden boat that I had stolen didn't stand a chance.

I could only think of one thing to do.

I pushed myself up and half ran, half stumbled across the deck and jumped over the railing into the churning water.

My hands grasped at the rope between Min and the yacht railing, burning with friction as I fell still holding it, and then it snapped. I kicked as hard as I could to keep my head above water, my hands pulling at the rope until it became taut. I pulled until Min's drenched body came up to mine.

The glowing water of the lake moved like an ocean in a storm. The magic hit me as if I was trapped in a burning house—exactly how I'd felt while rescuing Nadia that morning, only a thousand times worse. I swam toward the bobbing wooden boat, pulling Min along.

Another gunshot sounded in the air. Reuben didn't have any other targets but Blake. With the tumultuous water, could he have missed?

As Blake told me later, Reuben didn't miss. Blake didn't believe in magic, and he'd only followed my lead with Reuben's gun aimed at his head, but he had taken part in the ritual of Waking the Waterfall. For a moment, he had magic, and the journal with the protection spell on it had stopped what would have been a fatal bullet.

When the movement of the waves made the yacht lurch, Reuben missed his next shot by a hair, and the bullet only grazed Blake.

Meanwhile, I'd reached the smaller boat, still lashed to the yacht. I kicked and jumped, reaching for the side of the wooden boat with one hand, still hanging onto Min with the other.

I caught the boat's side and it tipped, filling with glowing magic water. I pushed the edge beneath me and, choking, hauled Min into the boat with me.

I rolled Min onto his back, as flat as I could manage inside the boat, and pushed down on his chest as hard as I could for a moment then released it. Again. I imitated his heartbeat.

"Min, you are not going this way!" I shouted at him. "Not because of me or my family secrets! And definitely not because of Reuben Connors!"

I leaned over Min's face, pinched his nose, covered his mouth with mine, and breathed into his lungs.

I drew a fist back and punched Min in the chest.

The lake went dark.

Min coughed and sputtered, then turned aside and vomited water. He pushed against the bottom of the boat with the heel of one hand and sat up, almost panting with panic. "Cath!" he gasped. "You saved me!"

I was so happy he was still alive that I kissed him.

"Stay here," I told Min, climbing up the yacht's ladder again as the waves calmed down. "I've got to take care of Reuben and Blake."

Blake shut the handcuffs with a snap. Reuben was now cuffed to the yacht railing.

"Blake!" I shouted, seeing the deck drenched with blood. The moonlight made the red fluid look black.

"You have the right to an attorney..." Blake persisted faintly. I shoved him a safe distance away from Reuben.

"Blake, you're bleeding really badly."

Blake stumbled, almost fainting. I put both my hands over his wound, trying to staunch the bleeding. "Hang on! Hang on, please! Stay with me. Jake and Talbot and everybody—they're on their way." They couldn't have missed that giant magical pillar of light, and they'd be curious about it.

"My heart's in your hands," Blake said faintly. "There are worse ways to die."

"You are not going to die," I told him. I knew it was a bad sign that Blake was getting so maudlin, though. "We saved the town. We saved Min! You don't do something like that and then just die. You just have to stay with me, all right? Blake?" He was looking at me, but his eyes seemed to glaze over. I called out to him again, "Blake!"

Reuben laughed, still struggling against the handcuffs and spewing threats that made no sense. My hands kept the pressure on Blake's wound until the police boats came.

26. One Loose End

J ake drove me home. I had some leftover pancakes for dinner, chewing ravenously as I called Bea to tell her the Order's devious plans had been thwarted. After that, I took a hot shower, slept without dreaming, and woke without Treacle.

With the Brew-Ha-Ha still closed, I didn't know what I would do. Still, I didn't feel like curling up in bed and replaying the horrors of the past three days in my mind. I also felt as though I was coming down with another case of magic burnout. It wasn't as awful as I'd anticipated after doing a spell as huge as Waking the Waterfall, but Min had given his life force—if only temporarily—and therefore did most of the magical heavy lifting.

Blake had said the ritual with me. I hoped the spell hadn't taken too much out of him, either. He would need his life force to, well, live.

I didn't know who to call first, so I decided I'd go to the animal shelter, make a donation, and thank some of the strays personally for all their help the night before. Maybe that would bring me back down to earth and clear my head.

The old man who ran the animal shelter, Murray Willis, turned out to be related to young Cody, from the insurance office. I found that out when I arrived to see a whole crew of news reporters filming an interview with Cody for a TV spot.

Old Murray was beaming with pride. As we doled out kibble into serving dishes, he chatted about how Cody had been studying bioluminescent flora and fauna in the Wonder Falls lake. "Glowing animals," Murray said, "too tiny to see just one. You can't even pet 'em! I never understood it."

I stroked a long-haired calico cat with a missing eye, and I said that understanding Cody's fascination was beyond me, as well.

"I would have wanted to be where you were last night, though."

I didn't know what to say to that. "Seriously, Mr. Willis?"

"Without the life-threatening hostage taking, o' course," Murray corrected himself. "But that bioluminescent pond weed made the falls glow brighter than a lightning storm. Think about that!"

"Oh, yeah," I said. "Nature's wonderful. Too bad people try to get in the way, right?"

"Folk like us and Cody just do our best," Murray replied. "And Samberg—is he out of the hospital yet?"

"I don't know. You know Blake? Detective Samberg?"

Murray nodded. "He's my most enthusiastic volunteer here at the animal shelter. It would be a pity if we lost him, and he hasn't even been a month in this town!"

The animal shelter didn't have a lot of volunteers. I decided to drop by more often, not just when I had to pick Treacle up again for wandering away.

At that moment, Bea called me on my cell. "Have brunch with us!" Bea said. "We're at the Parks' place."

"Still?"

"Of course we are. Mrs. Park wouldn't let us go off at—what, two or three in the morning? And with Mom just out of the hospital! Besides,

Min's here, and"—Bea lowered her voice—"he's really eager to see you again."

I smiled. "That wasn't some overwhelming trauma, then?"

"You're his hero! He doesn't mind the broken ribs. Mrs. Park and Mom have been catching up."

At that, I gasped. "Aunt Astrid's alive! I mean, awake! Awake and talking!"

"Go," old Murray told me.

I hung up the phone. "Thanks, Mr. Willis!"

"Thank you!"

I ran out past Cody and the news crew and uphill to the Parks' home. The townsfolk had found a cover story for the giant magical display of the night before, and they found it all by themselves. Aunt Astrid had come back to us. The sun was shining. Things were looking up.

When I saw smoke rising from somewhere near the Parks' front porch, I had a moment of panic, I admit, what with this town having had two suspicious fires in three days.

I only saw Mr. Park at the barbecue, though, which was surprising. He nodded a greeting and waved with the hand that wasn't flipping a burger with a spatula. I waved a greeting as I jogged toward him, noting the rest of the group gathered at a giant wicker porch table. Treacle was sharpening his claws on one of the table legs.

I was focused on stopping him, which was why I didn't see Min break away and come toward me. I jogged right into his cracked ribs.

"Oww!"

"Min! I'm so sorry!"

Min laughed and hugged me. "Worth it!"

We eventually broke apart, but we still couldn't quit grinning at each other. I craned my neck to look at the table. "What a crowd!"

Mrs. Park set down a tray of lemonade and beckoned me over as Bea followed up with a stack of paper plates and biodegradable plastic cutlery. I knew they were biodegradable because Aunt Astrid exclaimed at it, telling Mrs. Park, "You know me too well!"

Astrid really did look fully recovered. She turned back to chat with Jake.

"Detective Williams joined us only ten minutes ago. Other than him, our place was packed last night," Min said.

I watched as Jake nodded and waved goodbye at everyone. He gave Peanut Butter a rub under the chin on his way toward us.

Min continued, "Bea brought her mom and all three cats up here to comfort my mom while I was… you know…"

"Our families have always been so close," I said, hoping he wouldn't say how weird and unlike Bea that action was. I also hoped that if Min didn't get a chance to say it, he wouldn't get a chance to really think it through and get suspicious about it.

"Mom wouldn't let me go back to the inn room where I got kidnapped." Min gave an embarrassed shrug. "So it was a bit crowded. We still missed you, though!"

I grabbed Min's hand. "The last three days might have been hell, and I know you don't have good memories of this town to begin with, but I swear, it's not usually like this. How long can you stay—so that we can catch up?"

"I can stay as long as it takes for us to get properly caught up." Min said, "Besides, not all my memories of this town are bad."

"Cath," Jake said to me.

"I guess you need a statement or a testimony or something?" I said to him.

"I'll go get my dad to put something on the grill for you," Min said by way of excusing himself. "We've got burgers, hot dogs, and sausages—oh, and Mom made her pork-sausage patty mixin's, so—"

"That last one! I want that! Two of them, please," I called to Min as he headed for the grill.

I walked Jake to the police car down the slope, afraid of what he had to say. Aloud, I begged, "Tell me that Blake made it."

Jake said, "He's fine. It's not the first time he's survived a bullet to the heart, even. He told me so."

I sighed with relief.

"The doctors had to keep him sedated so he wouldn't try to work. Today! Can you believe that?"

"From Blake Samberg, I'm not surprised!" I laughed. "What's the Wonder Falls Police Department going to do with someone like that?"

Jake answered, "Well, lately I've been wondering what we'd do without him. His testimony, though… his and Mr. Park's…"

They'd both heard me admit to Reuben that I was a witch. "Reuben had me at gunpoint," I said to Jake. "He obviously believed that this old spell book, the prize of Aunt Astrid's collection, was real for some reason. But he had a gun on me! So I tried to play along."

"Blake believed that the three of you reading aloud from the book was what caused the lake to light up."

"Coincidence." I said, "I just came from the animal shelter. Cody was telling this news crew all about what happened last night—with the glowing, I mean. Of course, Cody wasn't at the standoff. Maybe when Blake's recovered a little more, he'll think more sensibly."

Jake persisted, "Min Park said that he had a vision of this goddess in the lake."

"Of course he would! He'd just had a near-death experience."

"Isn't his family Buddhist?"

I shrugged. "Last night was just confusing. By the way, when can we have that book back?"

"We have to hold it as evidence, unfortunately, until after the trial. It could be months before we can release it. It's obviously valuable to your family, but I've already bent too many rules. The chief has filed it as evidence with the justice of the peace. Someone would notice that it was gone. I'm sorry."

You don't even have the slightest hint of how sorry you should be! If that book falls into the wrong hands...

Almost as if he'd read my mind, Jake told me, "If there were a way I could get it back to you, you know I would. It's safer with your family."

I looked at Jake, startled. Bea couldn't have told him. But he'd figured something out. I told him, "It's just an old book."

"Really?" Jake said, in a tone of voice exactly between dismissive and challenging. Then he put the palm of his hand to his head. "Oh, would you look at that. You've been answering all my questions, and here I am without a notepad. We'll talk later, once you've thought through what happened last night. Right?"

I nodded.

"I'm off to follow up with Nadia LaChance," Jake said. "Reuben Connors and Dexter Edison haven't been cooperative."

"One goon got out alive, then?"

"Alive but behind bars. We don't have enough to implicate the entire Order, and Reuben Connors's alleged involvement with both fires… complicates things, especially in LaChance's case. But don't worry about the book."

Jake got into his car and drove away.

Not even three of Mrs. Park's pork-sausage patties, sandwiched in their respective English muffins, could get me to quit worrying about the book.

"Oh," I said when Min asked me what was wrong, "it's just that one of my aunt's most valuable pieces of a collection was stolen." He'd been showing me a slideshow of his trip to the south of Spain, and I think I might have confused an autopilot response to pictures of a bead shop with an autopilot response to the pictures of fountains that functioned somehow without modern pumping technology.

Aunt Astrid heard me and complained, "The police might as well have done the stealing if they don't give it back. Months, he said! Months!"

"Luckily," Bea added, "everyone who's deluded enough to think it's real is behind bars."

Min said, "Right!" sounding as though he meant it. "For today, for right now, everyone's safe. All's well in wonderful Wonder Falls."

Mr. Park said, "Show them the video of the Bali beach—the kites that were shaped like boats and look as though they're floating in the blue sky!"

So the records of Min's travels continued. Sunlight through the canopy of some African jungle. A performance of *A Midsummer Night's Dream* in some park in Australia, invaded by a swarm of giant bull ants. Beautiful stray cats in the Coliseum in Rome. A few more.

When it was done, I applauded. "It's great you got to see the whole world! Thanks so much for sharing it with us."

"Not that great," Min said. "You still take yourself with you, you know."

Bea said, "But you've changed! I mean..."

Mr. Park finished Bea's sentence, "You've grown. My boy's a man."

Mrs. Park disagreed. "He'll always be my baby."

I'd meant what I said about the rest of the world being great to see, especially through Min's perspective. His whole slideshow made me appreciate my own hometown that much more, though.

On the walk back to Aunt Astrid's place, Bea had a suggestion. "We should go camping."

We took turns carrying Marshmallow, as the old cat demanded. Peanut Butter didn't mind walking as long as he was with us. Treacle didn't mind wandering off and disappearing entirely.

But Treacle, with his scar, had been more loyal to me than any of the pudgy strays in Rome, with their unscratched coats, would have been. We didn't have playgrounds in Wonder Falls, but the kids could play safely in the meadows. Maybe one day I'd visit the mysterious jungles of darkest Africa or surf the magnificent and vivid tropical-blue waters of Balinese beaches, but I was in no hurry. We had enough mystery and magnificence in the waterfalls of my own little hometown.

"We haven't gone camping in years," Aunt Astrid said as we arrived at her place. She opened the door and went inside. "That would be lovely."

Bea set Marshmallow down on the sofa and followed her. Marshmallow scratched her ear with a hind paw and shook her head.

"So, when should we do it?" Bea asked.

I shut the door behind us and answered, "When this is all over."

Aunt Astrid nodded.

Bea looked from her mother to me, dismayed. "This isn't over? How can it not be over? Do you mean when we get our book back and can make sure that it's safe?"

"Yes. But also, I saw who attacked me," Aunt Astrid said. "It wasn't Reuben."

"Reuben Connors and that one guy aren't innocent in this whole thing," I said, as everything began to come together in my mind.

"But there's one loose end that we have to tie up, and we can't involve the police." I paused. "Well, maybe Jake. I think he knows, but I think he doesn't want to know."

Aunt Astrid said, "I'll put the kettle on, and Cath can tell us all about what she's figured out."

27. Uninvited Guests

The three of us met Jake that evening at the Night Owl, where he sat across from the LaChance twins.

Bea approached them first. "Mind if I get my husband back?"

"We're through here. Don't worry," Jake said to Nadia.

Nadia, uncharacteristically, was nearly in tears.

Jake continued to comfort her. "Reuben Connors is not going to bother anybody in this town anymore."

"But if you don't have a solid case, he could walk!"

"Deal with that when it happens," I said to Nadia. "For now, have you got a place to stay?"

Naomi answered for her. "She's staying at my loft. I just had to drag an extra mattress out for the top bunk. I only got a bunk bed because I liked four posters with the curtain that goes all around it, but it's turned out to be useful."

Nadia said, "I would have taken the sofa."

"Oh, please, as if that would have helped!" At my confused expression, Naomi elaborated: "Ruby Connors thinks she's too good for either."

"That's not true," Nadia objected. "Ruby just had to attend to another one of Darla's attention-sucking vortex phases. I'm sure I've got friends who irritate her, too."

Nadia caught my eye for a moment and then looked away.

Bea asked Nadia, "Are you and Ruby breaking up?"

"No!" Nadia almost shouted. "Not over something like this. Especially not after yesterday!"

"We'll see," Naomi said in a singsong voice.

Bea sat in the front passenger seat of the car as Jake drove. Aunt Astrid and I sat in the back with the Greenstone spell book between us. Jake had taken it from the evidence room.

Bea said, "You put a lot on the line for me and my family, Jake—"

"Don't mention it!" Jake said tersely, "Really, please—I love you, but… don't. Don't mention anything about this."

I expected Bea to look relieved, but she went quiet, her feelings quite hurt. I kept quiet, too. This was their marriage, and they'd have to figure it out themselves.

The police car pulled up to Darla Castellan's mansion, where Ruby Connors was supposed to be. We hid behind the bushes.

Jake rang the doorbell. From where I was hiding, with Bea beside me and Astrid with the Greenstone spell book on Bea's other side, I heard the door swing open and Darla ask what Jake wanted. There was a tremor to her usually steady, reedy voice.

Jake said, "Good evening. I was told Ruby Connors would be here. I just have some quick follow-up questions about yesterday's fire. They're sort of urgent."

Darla sighed and laughed. "Ruby! Detective Williams wants to talk to you!" She asked Jake, "Do you want to come in?"

"No," Jake said, "out here would be fine. I'm in a bit of a rush to get back to the station. I hope you don't mind. My interrogation with Nadia LaChance went on for longer than scheduled. She was upset."

"Look," Darla replied, "I might not have had my home invaded and burned down, but considering that nobody close to her just died, I think Nadia could be more respectful of people's time. Especially model members of the community such as yourself."

"It's no trouble."

Darla continued, "I mean *model* members of the community. You're quite the hunk, if I can say so. Like, you could be a model."

"You've said so before, ma'am, at which time I reminded you that I'm a married hunk."

I spared a glance at Bea, who was staring daggers at Darla.

Darla crooned, "Are you sure you don't want to come inside?"

At last, Ruby came to the door and followed Jake out to the courtyard. They passed by us without Ruby noticing.

"Now," I said, and the three of us started moving.

Darla had lingered too long in the doorway. Her face turned to outrage when she saw us approach, but Astrid opened the book. "You know what this can do? Just nod."

Darla nodded.

Bea said, "Unlike you or the Order, we actually know how to use it, so get back inside quietly."

"And we'll work something out," I added.

Aunt Astrid's expression softened. "I don't want revenge for attacking me, Darla. None of us want that. We just want some peace of mind."

With a resentful glance at our ruse—Jake was spinning his questions at Ruby in the courtyard, neither of them thinking to look over at us— Darla let us in.

28. A Collection of Little Bubbles

T he entire inside of her house smelled like artificial jasmine.

"First," I said, "what did we do wrong? How did we let on that we were witches?"

Darla shrugged. "Weird things always happened around you—ever since we were kids. When I got wise to the fact that you had something real but impossible going on, I thought that I was just lucky in school that you didn't have the spells to—I don't know—make me vomit sewing needles that I didn't remember eating. Then I thought, no, if they can do that, then they're the lucky ones!"

Bea's expression was a mix of contempt and horror. "You have a morbid imagination, Darla Castellan!"

"Witches do that," Darla insisted. Mocking Bea's tone, she said, "You're not the only one who reads, Beatrix Greenstone!"

"It's just Bea. And I'm a Williams now, by the way, so watch how you talk to my husband!"

"Oh," Darla said, "*you* can watch how I talk to your husband if you don't watch yourself—nerd!"

I got between them. "All right! You wanted magic powers. You've got failed businesses, courtesy of Winnifred Hansen. A failing marriage. You thought that a magic spell would solve all your problems in life, and you knew that we had magic."

Darla nodded. "I also knew that you wouldn't tell me. Selfish!"

Aunt Astrid looked hurt. "I gave you a tarot reading about your love life. I told you what you needed to compromise with—"

Darla scoffed. "Oh, please! That so-called marriage was dead in the water. Besides, if you have magic and you still continue to pretend that you've got life so hard—then you're obviously wasting it."

I said, "You've got wiles. Ted fell for them." It wasn't a question. "Fatally." That must have been what Reuben meant by a treacherous woman.

"It was the only way I could get him to tell me anything. Ted knew real magic when he saw it," Darla answered as she sauntered over to an armchair. "But he was afraid of it because of his mother. Years ago, before we got together, Ted found the trapdoor. He thought he would remind your Aunt Astrid of it to make a wine cellar—"

"I remember that," Astrid said. "It broke my heart to stop a Frenchman from caring for his favorite wines…"

Darla waved a hand dismissively. "He didn't mind! He thought that he'd sneak some racks and bottles in anyway. But he found the book hidden in the fuse box, and he got all scared! That coward! It wasn't even real. But he wouldn't even tell me where your Aunt Astrid's cellar was. The Brew-Ha-Ha was the last place I'd think of looking. I thought it was in some secret cabin out in the woods." She paused. "Don't think I only used him. I liked the guy, all right? I'd surprise him on the way to work in the early morning. We could have carried on for a long while, I can tell you. I sometimes even forgot to pick his brain about you!"

Bea shook her head. "A torrid, star-crossed romance, I'm sure it was. What a tragedy it had to end!"

"And what," I asked Darla, "reminded you to pick his brain about us?"

Darla answered, "Four days ago, I met Ted as usual, early in the morning, before he started prepping the dough or whatever. That morning was different because I heard something in the restaurant area, where nobody was supposed to be."

The legacy journal that had belonged to Blake's father had a locator spell on it. The Order must have used something similar and sent someone to the café in search of the spell book.

"Which member of the Order found the book?" I asked.

"I don't know," Darla said. "He had a stocking over his head when he came out of the cellar. Ted grappled with him and told me to run. The thief had dropped the book first. I picked it up, and then I ran."

"Ted was fighting for his life! But you cared more about what you could get—the book!" Bea accused.

Darla rolled her eyes. "He was still alive when I saw myself out. And Ted had told me to run."

I imagined the necklace worn by a member of the Order getting ripped from his neck in the struggle. Ted could have pulled off the stocking too, revealing... Reuben? Dexter? Felix? It didn't matter.

"It was supposed to be a simple theft," I said, "but they'd run into a witness instead. They couldn't leave Ted alive, and without the book, they couldn't wipe his memory. So they killed him and set the place on fire to destroy the evidence. But the cellar kept the footprints. I also caught a whiff of your perfume."

"I feared for my life, in every sense of the word!" Darla exclaimed. "My love life, my business, my reputation in this town were all in jeopardy—and now there was this group of strangers prepared to murder! I needed magic, but all I had was the fake book!"

Astrid nodded. "You'd seen what these people were capable of and thought that you needed to step up your game. You came into my home, armed with a baton, and demanded the real book. I wouldn't give it to you."

Darla was vehement. "I had to take it, so I did!"

"But," Astrid said, "you didn't know what to do with it. You only knew that it was powerful."

"And," I added, "you might have suspected that these strangers you were up against had magic of their own."

"So you foisted it off on your best friend," Bea said, "probably your only friend—Ruby Connors."

"It must have been hard," I said, "to outgrow unhealthy friendships and break away when she didn't have a supportive family. Ruby would let you use her because she thinks that's what loyalty means. How much of all this did Ruby know about?"

"Nothing," Darla replied. "I come and go. Sometimes I leave things. I'd been staying overnight at Ruby's place a lot anyway since Darren served the divorce papers. Nadia hates it, but that book would be 'just another one of Darla's things.' I read a little, and I hid it under the floorboards of the guest bedroom. I didn't dare use the book yet, but I figured that if I kept it hidden and safe, it could be a point of negotiation if they came after me."

"But," I added, "you wouldn't be safe if you tried to keep the book safe with you."

"Obviously!" Darla scoffed. "But I'm not a bad person, especially not to my friends. I knew Ruby would be better off joining me on a shopping trip. Besides, I figured that Naomi would give them enough trouble if they tried anything, but she folded too quickly, and they got the book back anyway."

"Nadia," I corrected.

Darla drawled, "Yeah, yeah. They look the same."

"They look nothing alike!"

"They're twins!"

Bea was shaking her head disapprovingly. "I wish that I could see you sorrier about Ted," she told Darla, "but you're not the one who knocked him out and set him on fire. Afterward, though, you could have killed my mother! You could have gotten our friends killed! You're no better than the agents of the Order."

"Oh yeah?" Darla said. "They're in prison. I'm not. And you're not going to put me in prison, are you?"

Bea and I exchanged looks.

Astrid nodded. "We didn't bring Detective Williams here to arrest you, no. That would be too conspicuous."

Darla gave a laugh. "I knew it!"

Bea seethed with rage. "Is that seriously how you defend your unconscionable behavior? 'I didn't get caught, so it must not have been wrong'?"

"We all do what we have to." Darla leaned back. "And you have to deal with me."

I nodded. "You're absolutely right. We need the fake book back. We're going into hiding again, so we've got to swap the real one with something that can safely sit in the evidence room of the Wonder Falls Police Department."

"And," Aunt Astrid added, "show up on trial as Exhibit A or so-and-so alphabet letter."

I forced my voice to sound cajoling, even flattering. "It would be such a huge favor to us, Darla. You wouldn't believe—"

"How about this." Darla wasn't amused. "I'll give you the fake book. You give me the real one, which I don't know how to use, and you teach me magic. But I'll keep the book with me."

"Done," I answered.

Bea backed away in horror. "That's not possible! Magic comes from the soul, and you, Darla, don't have one!"

At that, Darla stood up. "Just try me! Yeah, come at me, copperhead."

Bea peered at her. "Have your insults matured at all since grade school?"

Aunt Astrid cleared her throat, drawing attention to herself. "The other book, if you please?"

As Darla stood and went over to the coffee table, Astrid handed me the real book—which I held open—and Bea turned to the right page.

Darla returned with the fake spell book, which Aunt Astrid received gently with a smile.

"All right," I said. "Now we teach you magic."

We used the only spell in the book that didn't call for something as cruel, criminal, and unsanitary as a human sacrifice—although the three of us who did the spell would suffer magic burnout for weeks. Good thing we wouldn't need our magic for a long time to come.

As the witch whose magic dealt most closely with the mind, I tuned into the otherworld and began to pick out Darla's memories. With the help of Aunt Astrid and Bea, I had the energy to make new ones for Darla. We made Darla forget that she'd ever believed in magic at all, let alone in our magic. She'd never become interested in Ted. She'd had nothing to do with the attack on Ruby's place.

Darla Castellan would get away with everything she had done because we took it away from her. Part of me wished she could have been taken to task instead, for Ted's sake, but beyond her mind, I could see her heart, which was entirely the wrong shape for accountability. She'd always been a bully.

In the otherworld, the memories were like a collection of little bubbles. The ones I removed faded into wisps, like foam under a waterfall.

29. The Beginning

We sneaked back into Jake's police car before he and Ruby parted ways—Bea in the front passenger seat, Aunt Astrid and I in the back, just like before—except we had two books between us.

I kept an ear out. When Darla opened her front door, she exclaimed, "Ruby! What brings you here?"

Ruby only remarked, "Married guys aren't my type. Or any guys, really."

Darla whined, "That's so hurtful of you to say! In case you forgot, it was Darren who cheated on me first."

"I didn't forget," Ruby told her. "But I know you still want to tell me all about it again. Of course I'll listen, but—"

Then the front door shut, and their voices became too distant and muffled to hear.

Jake revved the engine and drove us back home. He took the fake spell book back to the evidence room, and Aunt Astrid took the real spell book somewhere even Bea and I didn't know.

Blake recovered from his gunshot wound just in time to give his testimony in court. When testifying, both Blake and Min seemed to have decided for themselves that the glowing water was indeed a coincidence. My confession about the Greenstone magic heritage wasn't even mentioned, only referred to as "Cath tried to play along" or "Cath tried to talk sense into him."

The Order denied having any part in the incident, but even the coverage in a small town like Wonder Falls proved to be too much scandal for them to handle. The fraternity dissolved, and the jury sent Reuben Connors off to an asylum for the criminally insane. Dexter Edison would serve a sentence of eight years in prison.

Ted Lanier was laid to rest in Canadian soil. Min had offered to fund the memorial service in France, but considering how much Ted had wanted to escape his old life, Aunt

Astrid arranged a small, quiet ceremony. I was surprised at the number of flowers laid on Ted's gravestone after that, considering Darla had completely forgotten him. Nobody else had expected her to remember.

We put a framed picture of Ted on a memorial wall in the new and improved Brew-Ha-Ha. Business slowed down due to the pastries from the Night Owl being unequal to Ted's and our being short-staffed in the front of the house. It leveled out fine in time, though. Any improvements we'd planned after rebuilding would just be a month or so later.

During what had always been the slowest time of the year for the Brew-Ha-Ha, we closed up for three days to go camping and fishing. We left the cats at the kennel even though Jake said that he wouldn't mind filling their dishes and cleaning their litter boxes. I didn't want him to follow an escaped Treacle into Greenstone Girls' Space, and the kennel seemed a more likely environment to keep the cats from wandering away.

As it turned out, though, there really was no stopping Treacle from going anywhere. He found our tents. So I let him have a jacket in my tent as a cat bed. I guess it would be a cat sleeping bag.

That night, Treacle woke me up again. He kept coming back to meow into my ear until I got up and followed him. It was a new moon's night, but my own magic let me tread unhindered through the forest. I could see with the sonic echolocation of the bats and find my way by starlight through the eyes of owls.

With my own human ears, though, I heard the rushing of the falls. I knew the way over the bridge.

That's where I met the Maid of the Mist. She stood on the bridge with me.

I know I saw her clearly, but I can't describe it now. My memory blurs in the strangest way, trying to remember if her dress was black or white.

"Well done," she said to me.

I gave a modest shrug. "I had help. I had my family—and Treacle, of course. I made new friends, too."

"That's all very important, and it wouldn't have happened if you hadn't played your part. It's been many generations since I've seen quite so much promise in a defender of this place, the falls between the worlds." She looked about my age, but my intuition told me I was in the presence of a being with years beyond wisdom.

"With all due respect, I can't make any promises. I should say that I appreciate you coming to meet me instead of speaking to me in a dream. This must be an honor of some kind, but I'm just sleepy. Unless this is a dream." I hugged myself, feeling chilled all of a sudden, and I rubbed my arms to warm them.

"Honor?" the Maid of the Mist echoed, sounding amused. "Necessity, maybe. You are a witch. You have bonds and duties. You will have more trials. Are you prepared?"

I took all that in and looked down at Treacle, who just looked back up at me. "Never," I replied. "I'm never prepared—but, you know, let me at 'em! When they happen, that is. For now, I think we all need to go back to sleep."

"True." With that, the Maid of the Mist dissolved. Treacle and I returned to the camp, where I first started writing all this out by flashlight.

I shouldn't be writing this down. I shouldn't have written it down. Those used to be the rules. I just feel as if I had to, though. Maybe it's because more is coming. The Maid of the Mist said so. A witch's work is never done, and I used to dread it. Now I embrace it.

I've started writing so I can remember this better and maybe so the next generation of Greenstones can be better prepared—or at least know they're not alone, even if I'm long gone.

My name is Cath Greenstone, I'm a witch, and this was the beginning. This was only the beginning.

About the Author

Harper Lin is the bestselling the author of *The Patisserie Mysteries*, *The Emma Wild Holiday Mysteries*, *The Wonder Cats Mysteries*, and *The Cape Bay Cafe Mysteries*.

When she's not reading or writing mysteries, she loves going to yoga classes, hiking, and hanging out with her family and friends.

www.HarperLin.com

CPSIA information can be obtained
at www.ICGtesting.com
Printed in the USA
BVHW030130020420
576660BV00001B/39

9 781987 859164